SERIOUS MOONLIGHT

Dave Turner

Aim For The Head Books

Aim For The Head Books
149 Long Meadow
Aylesbury, Buckinghamshire, HP21 7EB

www.daveturner.co.uk

ISBN: 9781838381028

THURSDAY

When you gaze into the abyss, the abyss also gazes into you.

You wave.

Then you realise the abyss was gazing into someone over your shoulder.

Awkward.

Invariably, it was gazing into Dave Marwood.

Dave was the hero London needed, but not the one it expected. If you'd asked for a show of hands from the population, few would pick the skinny guy with unmanageable hair. He looked like an assistant manager for a high street bank, but Dave was in fact employed by the Grim Reaper. He'd fought poltergeists and battled vampires. Only last week, he'd defeated evil forces controlled by a renegade Horseman of the Apocalypse trying to take over the global financial system.

Dave could talk to the dead, and they talked back. One thing dead people had in common was that they were annoyed that they were dead. As management wasn't available, Dave was the only person to whom they could address their complaints. And complain they did: every petty grievance they'd been unable to resolve in life; every regret; each lost love described in intimate detail. The afterlife really put things into perspective. He knew he'd be the same if left alone for decades with only the memories of every bad decision that led to his demise, so he always listened patiently and then helped them move on to whatever passed for the Great Beyond these days...

Which is why Dave lay in a shrubbery in one of the city's Royal Parks in the middle of the night. 'Is it the weekend yet?' he asked himself. While negotiating a rather high fence, his rucksack had caught one of the iron railings and he'd fallen into the foliage below with a crack of twigs. He crawled out, spitting leaves from his mouth, and brushed himself down. After unhooking the bag, Dave tiptoed across the pristine lawns and raked gravel pathways under an almost-full moon in a starless sky. The hum of spring in the city retreated behind him as he moved deeper into the park. Soon, all that broke the silence was the thwack-thwack-thwack of his flip-flops (look, it had been a boiling hot day, okay?).

A lone figure in running gear stared at a small bouquet taped to the branch of a weeping willow. Dave ducked behind a bush and unzipped the rucksack, taking out a black hooded cloak. When he'd pulled it over his shorts and tee shirt, the plastic Halloween scythe was next. Dave had cut the handle in two to make it easier to conceal in the bag and, when it had been assembled, he gripped it in a sweaty hand and took a deep breath.

'Let's do this', he whispered as he adjusted the hood to make sure his face was covered. He stepped back out onto the path and walked towards the figure with as much gravitas as he could muster.

'Matthew Avery?' he asked in a rough approximation of a booming voice.

The jogger turned around. He had a creased, doughy face as if it'd been over-kneaded by life. Dave estimated he'd been in his mid-fifties when he'd died. 'Yes?'

'I have come for you,' Dave said in a funereal tone.

'You took your time. I've been waiting here for hours wondering what I should do.'

'I apologise for the inconvenience.'

Matthew looked Dave up and down. 'You're not what I was expecting.'

'Is it my height? People always have a problem with that.'

'No,' replied Matthew. 'It's the flip-flops.'

'It's been very warm today.'

Matthew folded his arms. 'Is this some kind of wind up? Because I don't find it very funny.'

Dave sighed, pushed the hood back and smoothed his sweaty hair. 'No, this isn't a wind up. I'm very sorry, but you had a heart attack while jogging. My name's Dave. I'm here to help you pass onto the Other Side.'

'I was expecting the Grim Reaper, not the work experience kid.'

'He couldn't make it. He's having personal issues at the moment. I work for him. I'm just trying to pick up the slack as much as I can.'

5

'How does Death have personal issues?' Matthew asked, incredulous.

'It's very complicated.'

'I bet it is.' Matthew pointed at the cloak. 'Why the fancy dress?'

'I've found the newly dead expect a certain level of service. I thought trying to meet people's expectations might soften the blow.'

'How's that working out for you?'

'Badly.'

'So how did you find me?'

'I have alerts set up on my phone. I'm doing what I can, but I'm constrained by the laws of physics unlike others I could mention.'

'Where is he, then?'

Dave sat down heavily on a bench. 'At the bottom of a bottle, probably.' He pulled a chocolate bar out of one of the cloak's pockets and waved it at Matthew. 'Do you mind? I haven't eaten all day.'

Matthew shook his head. 'Go ahead. What happened to him?'

'You remember that kerfuffle over at UberSystems International a couple of months ago?'

'Riots? An entire building disappeared into a sinkhole? You don't forget something like that.'

Dave took a bite of chocolate. 'That's the story you heard, is it?'

Matthew shrugged. 'Well, there were a lot of rumours and conspiracy theories. Mad stuff, if I recall.'

'I was there. The conspiracy theories weren't mad enough.'

'Really?' Matthew asked. Not even death could stop interest in a juicy bit of gossip.

'It turns out the CEO, Conrad West - my old boss - was actually a Horseman of the Apocalypse.'

'What? Like the ones in the bible? Mr West? I met him once at a drinks function. He seemed quite nice,' Matthew said with surprise.

'Really?' Dave asked, spraying chocolate crumbs that passed right through Matthew. 'How'd that come about?'

'I work for MaxiFunds.' Matthew's face fell. 'I suppose I mean I *worked* for MaxiFunds.'

Dave smiled supportively. 'Yeah, the tenses get confusing in the afterlife.' Dave felt the phone in his pocket vibrate. He'd have to wrap this conversation up pretty quickly. 'Anyway, the short version is he'd summoned the tormented spirits of an eighties suicide cult and they, along with him, were banished from this reality, along with UberSystems Tower. We're not sure where they ended up, to be honest. So that leaves Death as the last of his kind. War, Famine, Conquest, they're all gone. He's taken it rather badly.'

'I find this very hard to believe.'

Dave shrugged. 'And a few hours ago you wouldn't have believed you'd be a ghost talking to a man dressed in a Grim Reaper costume he bought off the internet. Life moves fast.'

'Touché. I hope you claimed the outfit back on expenses. So, you're a medium?'

Dave twisted his neck round and tried to look at the label attached to the back of the cloak. 'I think it's a small, actually.'

'No, I mean you can talk to the dead?'

'Oh. Yes. Normally I don't deal with someone as... well... fresh as you.' Dave nodded towards the tree. 'Who are the flowers from?'

'Somebody from my office came and dropped them off a little while ago.'

'That's nice.'

'Is it? That's all I've got to show for my life. Some supermarket lilies bought with petty cash and an ex-wife who's already got her hands on my pension.'

Dave winced. He carefully slid his sleeve up and glanced surreptitiously at his watch. 'Well, I'd better get...'

'Fifty-three years and that's how it ends? Dead in a park? What's waiting on the other side?'

'I honestly don't know, but I've had no complaints from anybody so far.' Dave saw torch lights sweeping from side to side in the distance. He wiped his chocolate-smeared fingers on his cloak and stood up. 'I've got to be off now,' he said, nodding towards the approaching beams of light.

Matthew looked over his shoulder. 'Ah, right. Probably best to not be found in a park dressed like that at this time of night.'

'Exactly.'

'So, what happens now?'

'We just need to shake hands,' Dave said, offering his.

'Ah right. Goodbye, Dave. Thanks for the chat.'

Dave smiled. 'That's quite all right. Goodbye, Matthew.'

Matthew took his hand back. 'Perhaps you should talk to Death? Tell him he's dropped the ball on this.'

'Maybe I will. Thank you for your feedback.'

'Good. Things are always better after a chat.'

Dave and Matthew shook hands and, following a burst of light, Dave was all alone. He stood in contemplative silence.

Then, he ran.

☾

McHoan Gardens was the bustling hub of a new media industry. Digital marketing companies jostled for space with online branding agencies in the Victorian buildings clustered around a small green-fenced park. Behind the white-washed walls, bases were touched, paradigms shifted and goalposts moved. The road looping around the park was filled with expensively-dressed creatives moving from bar to bar. The weekend started early around here. Workmates and rivals shouted at each other under the sodium-orange streetlights: cheering, goading, synergising.

At the centre of all this energy, a dark figure sat quietly on a wooden park bench, drinking from a bottle. Nobody asked him to move on, or even gazed directly at him. He was a blemish to be ignored; an artefact on the surface of reality. Nobody except for Dave, who looked at him with a disappointed expression. The gate clanked as he opened it, but the figure didn't react.

'I thought I'd find you here,' Dave said. 'How long have you been sat there?'

Death shrugged. Dave huffed in frustration and sat down next to him, dropping the rucksack at his feet. Death offered Dave the bottle. *If you can't beat them, get drunk with them,* he thought, and took the bottle from Death's cold grasp. He wiped the neck with his tee shirt and took a long swig. Drying his wet lips with a sleeve, he passed the bottle back. They sat in silence as a heavily-bearded man unicycled past.

'How are they doing?' Death finally asked.

Dave flinched at the sound of his voice. 'Who?'

'Humanity.'

'They're getting by, as usual. Things are returning to normal.'

'How quickly they forget.'

Dave shook his head. 'Oh, they haven't forgotten. Everybody who saw what happened that night will remember it. It's like when you ask someone what they were doing when they found out JFK had been shot.'

Death shrugged. 'I was talking to JFK.'

'Okay, bad example. They all remember it, it's just that nobody wants to talk about it.'

Death took another slug of whiskey. 'How very British.'

When the UberSystems International CEO had disappeared into another plane of existence with the company's flagship offices, the remaining members of the board had decided not to ask too many questions and to cut their losses. The company was wound up and its assets sold off to rivals. The stock market had what is technically termed 'a bit of a wobble', but the traders soon had another crisis to distract themselves with. The staff, including Melanie, received generous severance packages upon signing a watertight non-disclosure agreement, which was fine by them as they didn't want to talk or think about that place ever again.

In the days that followed, life in London continued, everybody hoping nobody else would mention what went on during that night; millions of people suffering from collective embarrassment. They all ignored the hole ripped in the skyline. The city seemed to have developed a blind spot where the UberSystems Tower used to stand. The land was bulldozed and flattened, eradicating every trace, yet no buyer could be found. Some of the most valuable real estate in the world was left to lie fallow.

'How are you doing?' Death asked.

'Okay. I'm taking tomorrow off and going away with Mel for the weekend.'

'Anywhere nice?'

'The countryside. A break from London might be good.'

'They say when you're tired of London, you're tired of life.'

Dave gave Death as much side-eye as he could without giving himself a headache. They fell back into silence until Death waved the bottle at the buildings around them.

'We used to live there, you know?'

'Yes, I do,' Dave replied. 'What happened? Why did you move?'

'The usual problems that come with sharing a house. Arguments about keeping the kitchen tidy and borrowing each other's stuff. Oh, and the devil and a pan-dimensional being of unspeakable horror had a fight in the library and burned the place down.'

Dave nodded. 'Yeah, I had a similar experience with a flat share at university.' He took a breath and asked the one question he really wanted an answer to. 'When are you coming back to work? Perhaps it's time to get back in the saddle.'

'I'm not. You can sort yourselves out from now on.'

'That's it, is it? You're just going to abandon humanity?'

'What if I'm not needed anymore? Maybe that's why you and Anne have evolved the way you have. Maybe, over a few generations, you'll all be able to deal with it. The other Horsemen are dead, so what's the point of me?'

Dave snatched the bottle back and took another hit of booze. 'So, what are you going to do with the rest of eternity?'

Death thought the question over and then said, 'I always fancied trying golf. It can't be much different to swinging a scythe.'

'You can't just give up. I know you've had a bad time, but you've got to move on. You can't dwell on the past. You've got to keep moving forward to survive... like a shark.'

Death let out a loud, mocking laugh. 'And then get blown out of the water like Jaws at the end of Jaws.'

Dave turned to Death. 'The shark in Jaws was not called Jaws.'

Death returned his gaze. 'I think you'll find it was.'

'The shark in Jaws was called Bruce. I told you when we watched it that time.'

'No, you told me the puppet that played the shark was called Bruce. The character was called Jaws.' Death folded his arms. Checkmate.

'We're getting sidetracked. What I'm trying to say is the world depends on you.'

'You can't tell me what to do. You haven't been through what I have.'

Dave screamed internally. 'Oh, please. Stop this self-pity. You don't think people deal with this sort of thing every single day? That we don't all live with the weight of our own mortality on our shoulders, or deal with the relentlessness of everyday life?'

'I'm the last of my kind,' Death replied.

'So am I! My dad was killed by the stress of a job he hated. I watched my mum waste away and die in front of me. I have to say if you've only lost three people you care about in the thousands of years you've been moping around this planet then you've got off pretty bloody lightly. You reckon life is hard? Try being human.'

'That's how you feel, is it?'

'Yes, it is.' Dave sat back on the bench. 'Thank you for coming to my TED Talk.'

Death turned away. 'You should probably go now.'

Dave rolled his eyes. 'Oh, have I upset the great Death? The whisper on the lips of the damned? Is the dark companion who walks in the shadows of humanity's souls throwing his teddy bears out of the pram?'

'Just go.'

'Fine,' Dave spat, standing up and grabbing his rucksack. Death looked at it suspiciously.

'Is that a scythe in your bag?'

FRIDAY

Dave hunched over the steering wheel of a small hire car, his girlfriend Melanie in the passenger seat, heading towards the short break he'd surprised her with. He hadn't driven since moving to London and he'd negotiated the crowded city roads with what he considered to be a heroic lack of swearing. Soon the traffic thinned out and the choking grey streets gave way to green fields and wide skies. The further they moved away from the city, the more he felt the stress slip away. As much as he had grown to love his adopted home, he sometimes felt like the sheer weight of humanity would crush him. He stretched and relaxed into the driver's seat, pointing the car towards the open spaces in the north, and cruised.

'Are we nearly there yet?' Melanie asked, eager to get to their destination.

'If you carry on like that, I'm just going to turn this car around.'

Melanie groaned. 'Can't this thing go any faster?'

Dave glanced in the rear-view mirror. 'One of life's little pleasures is driving two miles per hour below the speed limit until the Audi driver behind you goes insane with rage.' Melanie turned around to look at the gesticulating motorist whose vehicle was almost touching the rear bumper of their car. She smiled.

'You are a terrible human being and history will judge you.'

Dave shrugged. 'You're the one who has to live with me.'

Melanie had moved in with Dave the day after they'd defeated Conquest. Her former housemate Emma had destroyed a large chunk of their flat while possessed by the restless spirits of the New Righteous Order of Armageddon, and that kind of behaviour just makes things awkward. This was the first time that either of them had lived with a romantic partner and they had soon learned that you had to compromise. Melanie understood Dave didn't enjoy reality television shows, so she recorded them to watch when he was out, and Dave discovered that Sitting-In-Your-Underwear-Watching-Television-And-Eating-Chicken Thursday wasn't a well-known pastime outside of his friendship with Gary. Their bedroom was a battleground upon which two opposing ideologies fought. Melanie's half of the room was tidy and organised; a place for everything and everything being in its place. Dave's looked as if a laundry basket had got drunk with a small public library, started a fight and then vomited all over the floor.

Dave took a hand from the wheel and covered his mouth, stifling a yawn.

'What time you get in last night?' Melanie asked.

'I don't know. After midnight. It was a fresh one. They're always the worst. Death hadn't shown up, so I filled in.'

Melanie sighed. 'You need to talk to him. It's not fair how you're being treated.'

'I did. It's difficult pinning down a being who hangs out on a different plane of existence, but I tracked him down.'

'How did it go?'

'I think I was a bit hard on him. He's having a bad time.'

'Well, the next time I see him, I'll give him a piece of my mind.'

Dave had to admire a woman happy to stare Death in the eye and tell him off. Melanie looked at the clock on the car's dashboard. 'We've been driving for an hour now. Are you going to tell me where we're going?'

Dave had decided it would be best to keep their destination a surprise, but now they'd left London behind he thought it would be fine to tell her. He was pretty sure she wouldn't throw herself from a moving vehicle, no matter how slowly he was driving. 'We're going to the Half Moon Inn in a village called Lunbridge. It's all very rural and tranquil. Rolling hills. Farmland. Long walks through the woods. Bucolic splendour. That sort of thing. You'll love it.' Melanie picked her phone up from the car's central console. 'What are you doing?' Dave asked.

'I'm seeing what the reviews are like.' Her thumbs skipped nimbly across the screen's keyboard. She read the webpage in silence before crying out, 'You devious sod!'

Dave tried to glance at the phone's screen. 'What?' he asked innocently, then winced as Melanie read from the hotel's website.

'"The hotel's owner, Martin, welcomes you to the Half Moon Inn in the peaceful and picturesque Lunbridge. Dating back to the sixteenth century, the building has played a central part in the history of the village and is full of charming character.

"As well as offering five-star service, the Half Moon Inn is internationally famous for being one of the most haunted hotels in the world. Will you see the Faceless Woman of Lunbridge in the east stairwell or the ghosts of the doomed lovers while relaxing with a drink in the saloon bar?"' She waved the phone at Dave. 'Did you know about this?' Dave's mouth flapped up and down in a non-committal manner.

Melanie folded her arms. 'This was supposed to be just the two of us. No work, no emails, nobody trying to kill us, turn us into the undead or drag us into parallel dimensions.'

They drove in silence until Dave said, 'Look, there probably aren't even any ghosts. It's a marketing gimmick. Anne asked that I have a quick glance around the place when we're there. It won't take long. We can have a nice break, chill, and, before we leave, I'll have a quick supernatural tidy up if I need to. It's killing two birds with one stone. In fact, it's easier than that because some of the birds are already dead.'

After a while, Melanie sighed. 'I suppose you're right. Just promise me it won't get in the way.'

Dave crossed his heart. 'I promise.'

Melanie relaxed. 'Good. Have we got anything to eat? I'm starving.'

Dave nodded towards the back seat. 'I made sandwiches. They're in my bag.'

Melanie leaned around her seat, pulled a plastic lunchbox from Dave's holdall and removed its lid. 'What is this?' she asked, removing a brown lump.

'A Crunch Cream sandwich. I invented it last week. It's a Crunch Cream biscuit sandwiched between two Chocolate Hobnobs.'

Melanie turned the supposed sandwich over in her hands. 'And how did you stick it all together?'

'Nutella.'

She nodded, understanding the concept but reserving approval. 'It's quite clever I suppose.' She took a bite. 'I take it back,' she said, spraying crumbs over the dashboard. 'It's genius.'

Dave laughed and steered the car onto the motorway, allowing the car behind to overtake. He waved cheerily in response to the very different hand gesture the Audi driver gave him. Holding Melanie's hand in his, he smiled to himself as he imagined that first drink in the beer garden. Yes, he felt bad about lying to Melanie, but she'd get over it and they'd relax and enjoy each other's company.

Yes, this would be a good weekend.

☾

Dave gripped the steering wheel tighter. 'Okay, so what do I do that annoys you?'

They'd been driving for nearly two hours and already argued extensively over whether a Jaffa cake was a cake or a biscuit. Dave had subsequently apologised for calling her a cake apologist.

'You always say thank you to Alexa when you ask it something,' Melanie replied. 'It will never acknowledge you. Why do you do it?'

'When the robot uprising starts, and they enslave all of humanity, perhaps the mechanical overlords will remember me being nice to her.' Melanie shook her head in disbelief and gazed out of the windscreen. 'And you never admit when you're lost,' she said. 'Why don't you ask someone the way?'

Dave had to admit that the bumpy, single-track road they were driving along probably wasn't the M4. The GPS on their phones had lost signal, and he'd been relying on instinct for the past few miles. He gestured to the grassy hillocks sloping away from the road on either side. 'Who? We've seen no one for I don't know how long.'

They passed a sign warning of a sharp bend. Dave slowed the car down as the verge on the left gave way to a cliff face that dropped away at a sickeningly steep angle. Harsh, unforgiving rock stretched down to the valley floor. Melanie peered over the edge, mesmerised by nature's cruel beauty beckoning her down onto the razor-sharp rocks below.

'Might just keep driving for a bit, though, yeah?' she muttered. As the car rounded the corner, she watched the drop disappear in the rear-view mirror. It was only then she realised she'd been holding her breath the entire length of the cliff-top.

Suddenly, over a slope, something fluffy and dirty-white lay in the road ahead of them, as if a rain cloud had crashed down from the sky. Dave brought the car to a halt, applied the handbrake and stepped out onto the road. Melanie followed him out and they both approached what they could now see was a sheep. The sun disappeared behind a cloud and a cold wind whistled through the valley. Melanie shivered with a chill that was more than meteorological.

The animal was dead, the darkening sky reflected in its lifeless eyes, a grey tongue poking grotesquely from its mouth. The remains of its throat were smeared across the rough tarmac and flies already danced at the edges of the wound.

'Must be a dog attack,' Dave said sadly. Melanie grabbed Dave's elbow.

'Let's get out of here.'

'Shouldn't we move it to the side of the road, or something?' Dave asked. Melanie's grip tightened.

'Let's go.'

Dave looked at the surrounding terrain carefully. Melanie's nervousness was contagious. 'Yeah, I think I can get the car around.'

☾

Dave and Melanie continued along the track in silence until they found the main road. Soon the signs pointed them towards Lunbridge and, after another ten minutes, they reached their destination. A poster advertising the Summer Fayre, scheduled for the following weekend, hung beneath the village sign.

'It's a shame we're not here for that,' Melanie said, pointing it out to Dave.

'It would be a fête worse than death,' Dave replied.

'This is what I have to look forward to for two days?' Melanie asked with a grin, dad-jokes a welcome alternative to the image of the savaged animal she'd been unable to shake from her mind.

Lunbridge itself was tiny. If you didn't pay attention, you'd drive straight through it. Tidy and well-scrubbed in the way English villages are, the streets were empty; a welcome change to the bustle of the city. Baskets of flowers hung from lampposts and hedgerows were trimmed into clean, geometric shapes. No harm could come to you in a place with such ruthlessly pruned shrubbery.

Dave felt that this was the sort of village where people pootled everywhere, so pootle along the high street they did. There was a post office, a florist, a shop that sold country wear, and little else. The phone signal was non-existent this far from the towns and cities, so Melanie had resorted to reading directions from a map Dave had printed out before they'd started their journey. Soon they reached the Half Moon Inn, situated at a crossroads where it had welcomed weary travellers throughout the centuries. It was whitewashed in a country style with small sash windows along its length. Dave turned the car into the car park, the gravel crunching beneath the tyres as he tried to reverse the car into a narrow parking space.

The car park backed onto a field where the crops were just sprouting and, beyond that, there were softly undulating hills carpeted with thick grass. Dave walked up to the fence at the edge of the village. Stretching his arms wide, he breathed deeply, filling his lungs with the warm, clean air, and then slowly exhaled.

Melanie, following behind, wrinkled her nose. 'What's that smell?'

'That's nature,' Dave replied calmly.

'It smells like your bathroom after Gary's used it.'

Dave's mood became somewhat dampened by the image as they returned to the car, grabbed their bags from the back seat and went into the hotel.

Disorientated by the sudden change from the bright heat of the day to the cool darkness of the bar, Melanie and Dave blinked and squinted until the room came into focus. The interior of the Half Moon Inn was where the countryside came to die. Lethal farm equipment hung from the low ceiling. Reproduction oil paintings of a bygone rural age hung upon the floral wallpaper and horses' brasses decorated the brown, beer-soaked bar. Half a dozen drinkers - farmworkers by the look of their grubby clothes and heavy boots - stopped their conversations mid-sentence and stared at Dave and Melanie.

Hello, we're not from around here. When's the witch burning? Dave thought as he smiled in the uncomfortable silence.

'Hi. We've got a room booked?' Melanie said.

A wiry, twitchy young man, in his twenties, pointed around the corner of the bar. 'Reception's through there,' he said in an accent so thick Dave thought he could grow potatoes in it.

'Thanks,' Melanie replied, and they walked through the pub, their footsteps loud on the floorboards as six pairs of eyes followed them until they were out of sight.

They passed through a doorway into a small reception foyer. Dave rang the bell on the desk for attention. He looked over at Melanie and, barely audibly, hummed the theme tune from Deliverance, which earned him a playful punch on the arm.

A middle-aged man appeared from the back office. He was squat and furry, with a heavy beard and thick eyebrows that met just above a wide nose. 'Welcome to the Half Moon Inn,' he said with a wide grin. 'My name's Martin. How may I help you?'

'We have a room booked. In the name of Marwood?' Dave said.

Martin turned to the computer and tapped a few keys. 'Ah, yes. You're in the Landis Suite. I'll just need a few details from you and then you can retire to your room.' He pressed another button and the printer sprang into life. 'And where have you come from today?'

'London,' Dave replied, caught in the bright headlights of small talk.

'Ah, the Big Smoke. You must be those Millennials I keep reading so much about. I must admit to raising hell in various boroughs of that particular metropolis in my youth.' Martin pulled the paper from the printer's tray and placed it in front of Dave in a smooth flourish. 'If I could just have your address and signature.' Dave wrote his details in a spidery scrawl.

'How is it after all that unpleasantness?' Martin asked.

'It's all fine now,' Melanie replied.

'Though I feel it's rather careless for you to lose an entire building. The last thing I read was that they believe it fell into a large sinkhole.'

'A sinkhole?' Dave repeated.

'Yes. A hole into which things sink,' Martin explained slowly.

'Well, it's a big place. We'll probably find it round the back of the Shard or something,' said Melanie.

Martin laughed politely as he took the paper back from Dave. 'Let's hope so. I can't say our little hamlet can offer such excitement as that.'

'I hear you've got ghosts?' Dave said, changing the subject.

'You have an interest in the paranormal?'

Dave shrugged. 'It's all right, I s'pose.'

'We are rather famous for our more ethereal guests. Have you ever seen a spook, spectre or spirit?'

'No, not that I know of.'

'Perhaps that will change this weekend. This whole area is known for its supernatural activity.'

Melanie nudged Dave with her elbow. 'That sounds interesting, doesn't it darling? You've always wanted to see a ghost.' She could barely contain the laugh that was bubbling up. Dave gave her a withering stare.

'In fact, we have a paranormal research team from the local university staying here,' Martin said, raising his eyebrow. 'Who knows what they might find?'

'They'll not be a bother, will they?' Dave asked. 'We've come for a relaxing weekend.'

'I assure you they'll keep out of the way. Now, could I possibly trouble you for a credit card in the event you charge any items to your room?'

'Of course.' Dave took his wallet from his back pocket and looked inside. He selected a card that could take one more for the team and handed it over.

Martin ran the plastic through the card machine and passed it back. 'There. All done. I'll just call Carter to show you to your room.'

He rang the bell again and a frail old man in a dark suit entered from the restaurant.

'You rang?' Carter asked in a tremulous voice.

'Could you show our charming guests to the Landis Suite, please?' Martin asked as he handed a key over.

Carter brushed his thin white hair back with gnarled fingers. 'With pleasure.'

He hobbled over to the luggage. Dave was worried that the weight of the cases would snap Carter's fragile arms off at the elbows. 'That's all right. We can manage,' he said.

Carter grabbed a heavy case in each hand and lifted them effortlessly. 'Nonsense. I wouldn't hear of it. Right this way.'

Melanie and Dave stared with open mouths as he climbed the stairs two at a time. Martin smiled, all teeth and rural hospitality. 'He likes to keep active.' He returned to his paperwork before looking up again. 'I'm very sorry. I hope you don't mind me saying, but you seem familiar. Have I seen you somewhere before?'

'No,' they both answered in unison, an instinctive reaction since the aftermath of the vampire attacks and their faces on the news.

'My mistake, then.' Martin nodded towards the stairs.

'Right. Thanks for your help,' Dave replied before he and Melanie headed up the staircase.

Through the doorway to the bar, the wiry young man watched them with hungry eyes.

☾

Melanie and Dave caught up with Carter as he listed from side to side along the dimly-lit corridor.

'The manager seems interesting,' Melanie said. 'What's his story?'

Carter stopped outside a dark oak door and placed the bags on the thick, grey carpet. He looked at them through milky eyes. 'Little is known about Mr Martin. Some say he's an angel. Some the devil,' he croaked as he rattled a key in the door's lock. The air crackled with meaning as the door swung open with a conveniently ominous creak. The hairs on the back of Dave's neck stood up. Then Carter shrugged. 'While others say he was a marketing executive who retired to the country. I wouldn't pay much heed to what people say around here,' he said as he grabbed the bags and waddled into the bedroom.

Dave and Melanie looked at each other, then followed Carter. Dave had seen nothing like this hotel room outside a haunted house movie. A large four-poster bed dominated the centre of the room and dark wooden panelling lined the walls. He gently pushed at each one.

'What are you doing?' Melanie asked.

'It looks like one of those places that would have a secret passage,' Dave explained.

Carter placed their bags on the ottoman at the foot of the bed and turned to the guests. He pointed to a door opposite the room's entrance. 'The bathroom is through there.' He then waved it towards a bottle in a silver bucket on top of the minibar. 'A bottle of champagne as you requested, Sir. Is there anything else I can help you with?'

'No, I think that's everything,' Dave replied. There was an uncomfortable silence as Carter looked at him, until Dave realised the part he needed to play in the transaction. He took his wallet from his back pocket, pulled a crumpled note out and handed it to Carter. 'Thanks very much.'

Carter palmed the note expertly, and it disappeared without a trace. 'And thank you, Sir. If you need anything, please don't hesitate to ask for Donaldson.'

'I thought your name was Carter?' Dave said.

'It is, Sir.' Carter turned to Melanie and gave a small bow. 'Madam,' he said before leaving the room.

'"The manager seemed interesting. What's his story?"', said Dave when the door had closed. 'You all right there, Agent Scully?'

Melanie shrugged. 'I was just seeing if we can get a little background information. Might make your job easier.'

Dave nodded to the bed. 'Do you wanna?'

Melanie gave him a sly smile. 'Yes.'

So, as is traditional when guests first arrive in a hotel room, Dave and Melanie threw their shoes off, jumped onto the bed and bounced up and down on the firm mattress. When he felt sick, Dave sat down and rifled through the drawers of the bedside cabinet. He pulled out a Gideon's bible and flicked through the pages. Stopping at Revelations, he pointed at a verse and said, 'I know that guy.'

'Do you want a cup of tea?' Melanie asked. Dave wrinkled his nose.

'Gary tells me that everyone goes for a wee in hotel room kettles at night.'

Melanie rolled her eyes. 'No, they don't. I reckon Gary goes for a wee in hotel room kettles and then just assumes that everyone else is as depraved as he is. Well, if you don't want a cuppa, I'm having a shower. I need to wash that journey off,' Melanie sighed. She slid off the bed and headed to the bathroom, leaving a trail of clothes as she went, a sly smile on her lips as she disappeared through the doorway.

Dave lay frozen on the bed. Should he follow her in there? Was that smile an invitation? He was notoriously bad at this kind of thing. But as he listened to the running water, he pictured it cascading down her naked body and decided to join her. This was a romantic weekend after all. He crossed the bedroom floor, frantically discarding clothes.

Steam fogged the bathroom. He stepped gingerly into the porcelain bath tub, careful not to slip. Melanie's reaction was one of pleasant surprise. They kissed, their hands running over their slick bodies. They lathered each other. Dave got soap in his eyes. Then he stumbled blindly, catching his leg in the shower curtain. He tried to salvage the situation by trying to give Melanie a smouldering stare through stinging eyelids, but it made him look constipated.

Avoiding Dave's floundering, Melanie elbowed the cold tap. The couple were deluged with freezing water, which finally killed off any remaining vestiges of passion. Dave sighed. He simply wasn't built for sexy. They rinsed themselves off and returned to the bed, which was territory he was far more familiar with. His confidence restored, they both put out their best moves and a few new tricks until they collapsed, exhausted, in each other's arms.

'Wow!' Melanie gasped, running a hand through damp hair. 'That was incredible.'

'Well, I have been practising on my own when you've been out,' Dave replied between panting breaths.

Melanie slapped him on the arm. 'Are you going to open that champagne?'

They alternated between drinking chilled wine and lazily making love for the rest of the afternoon. Dave's excitement increased when he remembered a biscuit assortment he'd packed in his holdall.

As he lay with Melanie amongst the covers and biscuit crumbs, Dave had never felt closer to another human being. Their nakedness exposed their scars and wounds to each other. He traced a finger along the curve of her jaw, enjoying the intimacy of the simple action, continuing down her slender neck and stopping at the two small puncture wounds she'd received while saving his life. The skin was rough; a permanent reminder of that night they almost died. A vampiric tattoo. A memento from a trip to a new existence. For reasons he couldn't fathom, he felt a pang of jealousy.

Melanie placed a hand on his, bringing him back to the present. 'What are you thinking about?' she asked.

Dave searched for something to say. He couldn't tell her the truth. 'Do you think the dress Leia wears in the Ewok village is from the last person they ate?'

'Your obsession with Ewok dietary habits isn't healthy.'

Dave rolled onto his back. 'I'll tell you what's not healthy; trying to eat Jedi.'

'Which reminds me, we should go down for dinner.'

Dave searched under the bed covers and found a Bourbon biscuit. 'I think this one is still good.'

'Something hot. It's getting late. We should go down to the restaurant.' The sky had turned a deep crimson; a blood-coloured gash in the gap between the drawn curtains.

They showered again, this time separately to maintain their dignity. Melanie had chosen a pastel summer dress and was applying her make-up when Dave walked back into the room, a towel wrapped around his waist. He went to the wardrobe, pulled out a shirt and put it on.

'You're wearing that, are you?' Melanie asked him in the mirror.

Dave looked down at the shirt he'd put on; a bright Hawaiian number. 'It's my holiday shirt. It says I'm here to relax, but I'm not afraid to party when required.'

He read Melanie's body language, her arms folded and face set like stone, and sighed. He'd learned from bitter experience that any question Melanie asked about his sartorial decisions should be answered with a resounding 'No': *Are you sure that tie goes with that shirt? Are those shoes practical enough for a walk along the South Bank? Do you think an AC/DC tee shirt is appropriate for my nephew's christening?*

Dave knew when he was beaten. He took the shirt off, put it on its hanger and back into the wardrobe. He chose a more conservative look and, once he had approval from Melanie, they finished getting ready and headed downstairs.

☽

The night was warm and spring-like so, after they'd finished their meal, Melanie suggested to Dave that they take a walk around the village. She let him complain for a while, killing time until he - having inevitably decided that he'd rather have an easy life - agreed to the idea.

'It'll be good to do something different for an evening. What would you be doing if we weren't here?' she asked as she sipped her coffee.

Dave shrugged. 'Gary was going to do a Die Hard marathon tonight.'

'All of them? Even the fifth one? Hardcore. That's actually quite heroic.'

'No,' said Dave, 'John McClane is the true hero because he met Ellis just once at a party in the first one and can remember his name a few hours later.'

'He's not as heroic as Keanu Reeves in Speed,' Melanie replied.

'Blasphemy.'

'He handles everything John McClane does while also dealing with a massive hangover.'

Dave nodded in agreement. 'That's a good point. Okay, let's paint the town red. Get your cardigan.'

The low sun struck the roughly-hewn white stone of the village's cottages, turning them a striking rust-orange. The scent of freshly-cut grass hung in the air and the moon appeared a translucent milky white as if projected onto the fabric of the darkening sky. To the couple's surprise, there was not a single other person on the streets. Everybody had shut them-selves away behind pretty wooden doors. The only building that seemed to show any signs of life was the small church they'd passed as they'd entered Lunbridge.

'Let's go inside,' Melanie said, taking Dave by the hand.

'Are you allowed to?' Dave asked, knowing she came from a long line of guilt-ridden Catholics.

'You agnostics don't know a thing, do you?' Melanie shrugged. 'Meh. It's Anglican, so it's like Diet Christianity.'

She led him along the gravel path and, pushing the heavy oak door open, entered the church. The cool, dark air hit them like a slap to the face. They walked down the aisle between the pews, their seats rubbed smooth by centuries of worshippers. The low sun shone through the stained-glass windows, illuminating scenes that featured more blood than Dave normally liked to see in a place of worship. There were beheadings, strange creatures eating bizarre animals and a group of really annoyed-looking Saints brandishing very pointy weapons.

'The artist was going for an Old-Testament-Wrath-of-God vibe, wasn't he?' Dave said, staring up at an intricately-designed image of a disembowelled sinner. 'The intestines really follow you around the room.'

'I see we have a gentleman who appreciates fine artwork,' said a voice from behind. Dave jumped in shock and his stomach decided that it had a pressing engagement with his ankles. He turned to find a round, jovial man wearing a dog collar grinning at the couple. 'I'm Reverend Peter. I'm sorry, did I startle you?'

'A little,' replied Dave. His stomach decided that the journey south seemed far too much like hard work and returned to its regular position.

'It's unusual to find visitors here this time of night. Are you staying at the inn?' Peter asked.

'Yes,' replied Melanie. 'We're up from London for the weekend. I'm sorry, should we not have come in?'

'The church is always welcoming. I see you're interested in our stained-glass windows. They're rather striking, aren't they?'

'That's one word for it,' Dave said. 'Was there a sale on red glass when they were made?'

Peter laughed politely. 'They depict various legends told of the local area. Unfortunately, a lot of claret gets spilled in them, as you Londoners would say. With all the tragedies that have befallen Lunbridge, there are many who say the village is cursed.' He pointed to the closest window where a black creature stalked an innocent child like a shadow, its sharp teeth bared as it prepared to pounce. 'This one tells the story of the Beast of Lunbridge. A young farm boy fell in love with the only daughter of the Lord of the manor. Knowing they could never be together, they begged a coven of witches to transform them into wolves so that they could live in the forest together.

'Enraged, the Lord led a hunting party into the forest with the intention of killing the male animal and forcing the witches to change the she-wolf back into his daughter. Dreadfully, in the confusion of the hunt, the she-wolf was slain, and the farm boy escaped deep into the woods. After the Lord had dealt with the witches, he spent the rest of his days hunting the wolf whom he blamed for the death of his daughter.

'Finally, the Lord and the wolf faced off against each other. They fought long and hard until, both at the point of exhaustion, the wolf tore the Lord's throat out. Now they say the Beast of Lunbridge still hunts these lands; all his previous humanity eradicated, preying on those that enter the woods.' The sound of thunder rumbled and rolled off the stone walls of the church.

'I'm very sorry,' Peter said. 'I've left the television showing a documentary about the rainforests on in the vestry. I do so love Attenborough.'

'Please, don't let us keep you from it,' Melanie said.

'Thank you. Feel free to stay and explore the rest of the church. It's so nice to have young people take an interest. There are so few parishioners who come here these days, what with so many heathen pursuits to catch their eyes.' The vicar subtly nudged a wooden collection box closer towards Dave. 'Yes. So few.' Dave took a five-pound note from his pocket and slid it through the thin hole in the top of the box. 'Oh, bless you, my child. I shall leave you two alone now, but if you need anything, please ask.'

Peter turned, walked back up the aisle and disappeared into a small office to the side of the building, closing the door and silencing the soothing words of

David Attenborough. Dave looked back up at the scenes in the widows and turned to Melanie.

'It's very important that I have a beer within the next ten minutes.'

☾

When they returned to the hotel, Dave and Melanie ordered drinks at the bar and took them out to the garden. The moment was perfect and still; the couple holding hands as they stared up in awe at the heavens. Away from the city lights, the moon was a large bright disc pressed against a dark sky hung heavy with the furnaces of a billion stars. Millions of them were already extinguished, constellations dying and burning out, the distance so great that only now the memory of their light was reaching the earth.

Dave wondered what would happen to Death now that he was the last of his kind. Would he be forced to walk the earth alone until the sun swelled and consumed the planet before shrinking away to a cool dark husk, or would his time come before that? Would he cease to exist along with humanity when there was no longer any need for his services? Dave debated whether he should text him, to let him know he was being thought of, but his phone had no signal.

An argument erupted amongst the group on the table next to them. There were three men and two women. Four of them appeared to be in their early twenties while the fifth, a middle-aged man with thin grey hair scraped back into a greasy ponytail, was obviously the leader around which the others had gathered.

'Nonsense,' he said to his small audience. 'The Enfield Haunting was obviously a poltergeist event of immense power.'

A young man pushed his thick-framed glasses up his nose with a finger and replied with a mocking laugh. 'It was a textbook example of a hoax magnified by investigators seeing what they wanted to see.'

Melanie leaned over to Dave and whispered, 'I'm guessing these are our ghost hunters.'

Dave raised his eyebrows. 'It would appear so.'

'Let's say hello,' Melanie said, a mischievous glint in her eye. Dave objected, but she was already out of her seat. 'Are you the ghost hunters from the university?' she asked the leader of the group. He winced.

'We prefer to call ourselves paranormal and parapsychological researchers,' he corrected her in a patronising tone.

Melanie pointed to Dave. 'My boyfriend saw a ghost once.' Five pairs of eyes swivelled round to face him. He waved sheepishly.

'Actually, I think it might have just been a white sheet on a washing line.' As one, the group let out a disappointed sigh. 'I'm sorry,' Dave said, unsure why he was apologising.

'I'm Brian. Would you like to join us?' the older man asked.

'Sure,' Melanie replied with a smile. Reluctantly, Dave dragged their chairs over and Brian introduced the members of his group. There was Griff and Jenny, third year history students, who Dave surmised were goths in love from their black clothing and clasped hands in the shadows under the table. Rick, the man with the thick-framed glasses, was an interloper from the university's skeptic group who'd been invited along to have his preconceptions challenged. Lila, a first year English student and the youngest of the five, hid behind her long blonde hair and hardly said a word. She quickly became Dave's favourite.

'Where are you from?' Brian asked, supping his foamy warm ale.

'London,' Melanie replied, bracing herself for the impact of the questions that would follow. Brian just sat back in his chair and wiped his damp fingers on the faded Ramones tee shirt he was wearing.

'Terrible what happened there last week. Baffling.'

'What do you think it was?' Griff asked, nervously tapping his pint of Guinness and Black with a painted fingernail.

Brian steepled his fingers together in contemplation. 'Parallel dimensions,' he said, finally. 'It slipped between a gap between our world and another.'

It surprised Dave how accurate Brian's guess was, but he kept quiet. Rick simply coughed. It sounded quite a lot like the word 'bollocks'.

'I heard it had something to do with sinkholes,' Melanie countered.

'Current thinking on some forums is that it was a controlled explosion,' Jenny said softly.

'What's the point of that?' Dave asked.

Jenny shrugged. 'UberSystems International were making inroads into the Chinese market, making deals with the government. Some powerful people were unhappy about that power grab.'

Melanie laughed. 'You should meet our friend Gary. You'd get on like a house on fire.'

'That would explain that false flag incident there a few months ago,' Griff said, warming to the subject.

Rick groaned. 'Who put fifty pee in the dickhead? False flag? You're really going there, are you?'

'False flag?' Dave asked against his better judgement.

Griff leaned forward, conspiratorially. 'When those workers supposedly died, nobody was ever arrested over it. It was a government hit job, probably to destabilise the company, but it didn't work so they had to step up their game. What do you think it was?'

Dave gripped the arms of his chair, his knuckles whitening. He wanted to reach across the table and punch the smug expression off Griff's pale face. With great control, he simply muttered, 'I wouldn't know about that sort of thing.'

Dave studied the patio's paving intently, examining the cracks in the slabs, half hoping one of these sinkholes might conveniently appear for him to slide down into. Melanie glanced over, concerned. Dave picked up his almost-full pint and drank it down in one. Coolly, he placed it back on the patio table and said, 'Oh, looks like I need another. Can I get anyone a drink?' Everybody shook their heads. Dave calmly stood up and went into the bar.

'Is he all right?' Griff asked. Melanie fixed him with a steely glare.

'We used to work at UberSystems International. We lost friends in that so-called false flag incident.'

Griff shrank back from Melanie's stare. 'Oh, God. I'm so sorry.'

Melanie's gaze didn't waver. 'He just gets upset when people reduce our lives to a conspiracy theory on the internet.'

☾

Shaking, Dave stumbled into the bar. He'd never be rid of this. For the rest of his life he would be linked to the madness at UberSystems International. Whispers, rumours and gossip would follow him wherever he went like a stench that caught the back of the throat.

Lost in that thought, he walked straight into somebody walking in the opposite direction. He jumped back in surprise and saw that it was the wiry young man who'd guided them to the hotel reception earlier on. Dave tensed. Bitter experience had taught him that his next action would be vitally important to how this would play out. He solemnly performed the traditional Ancient London Ritual of Apology and Remorse.

'Sorry, mate.'

The man gave him a lopsided, drunken grin; all teeth and good humour. 'No problem,' he said,

41

patting Dave on the shoulder. He continued past Dave, weaving his way between tables and out into the garden. Dave stood there, bemused. So, it was true. People were nicer in the countryside.

He found the bathroom. It followed the design of the rest of the building; dark wood and photographs of the village's past. He ran one of the sink's taps, splashing cold water on his face. He stared in the mirror as the rivulets of water ran down the lines of his reflection. He seemed so much older than the young man who had made his way to a Halloween party a few months ago.

He was calmer now. His breathing had regained its regular rhythm and his hands were steady as he ran them through his hair. As he dried them with a paper towel, he gazed at one of the sepia photographs on the wall. According to the picture's caption, it had been taken just outside the building in 1932. A group of what Dave guessed were the regulars of the day were gathered in the foreground where the car park was now standing. He smiled as he scanned the faces in the group. They seemed a fun bunch. Then he stopped smiling.

A lopsided drunken grin; all teeth and good humour, beamed out from the photograph. It was the man that Dave had just bumped into and he hadn't aged a day. Common sense said this was an ancestor, a great-great-grandfather, but the similarity was uncanny and common sense rarely showed its face in the world Dave now lived in anyway. He couldn't be a ghost, as Melanie could see him, and he'd been walking around in daylight, so that ruled out vampires.

This was something new. Something different.

☾

Dave ordered another drink at the bar. As the barman poured it, he searched the room but the young man hadn't returned.

'What's the name of the young guy who was here a minute ago?' Dave asked as the barman placed the fresh pint in front of him. 'Tall? About my age?'

The barman looked at him with suspicion. 'That'll be Tommy. Why are you askin'?'

Dave shrugged. 'I thought I recognised him, but I must be thinking of someone else.'

The barman looked Dave in the eyes. 'Tommy ain't never left the county, so I think maybe you must be.'

Dave returned the glare. 'Yeah, I guess so.'

He paid for the drink and returned to the garden where Melanie was still talking to the ghost hunters.

'Look, I'm sorry about what I said before,' Griff said as Dave took his seat. His mind on other matters, Dave waved the apology away.

'It's fine. Don't worry about it.' Dave leaned over and asked Melanie, 'Did you see that guy who helped us when we arrived come through here?'

'Yeah, he left. I guess he went home. Why? Is there a problem?'

Dave shook his head and sipped his drink. Melanie looked at him warily. He wore that familiar

43

confused expression; the one where he was trying to remember whether it was bin day, or the End Times. Knowing she wouldn't get an answer from him, she turned back to Brian. 'So, what are you researching tonight?'

'Ah, tonight should be very interesting, though it will have to go some way to beat our greatest discovery.'

'And what was that?'

Brian leaned forward so that his beard was almost dipping into his drink. 'We once watched a pencil roll over two inches along a desk.'

Melanie leaned towards him, mirroring his movements. 'All on its own?'

Brian nodded. 'All on its own. We have it recorded on video.'

'Wow!' Melanie said. Only Dave detected the playful sarcasm.

'Tonight, though, our research will be full of heartbreak and sorrow,' Brian continued, enjoying a new audience to perform to. 'In 1742, Ophelia Gilbert and Daniel Meacher fell in love. The offspring of two warring families, any relationship between them was forbidden by their parents. Unable to deny their passions nor forsake their families, a priest married them in secret. They ran away, stopping here for the night. When word got to them that their families had given chase and were mere miles down the road, they put poison to each other's lips and died in each other's arms safe in the knowledge they would be with each other for eternity. Now, their spirits haunt room 203. They say you can hear them call out to each other from the ethereal plane.' He pointed a finger at Rick. 'Don't you say a bloody word.'

Rick, drawn into Brian's story as much as the others, did as he was told. They all sat in silence, each of them contemplating the centuries Ophelia and Daniel had spent walking the line between worlds. Then, in the distance, an animal's howl sliced through the silence. The cry filled the vast space of the valley, wordlessly telling a story of pain and savagery. Dave couldn't imagine what sort of creature could make a noise like that, but it worried him.

'What was that?' Lila asked.

'It's just a dog,' Brian replied with confidence, though Dave could see that he was as unnerved by the sound as everybody else. 'Perhaps it's time we set our equipment up. It's getting late.'

☾

With growing disdain, Rick watched the University of Redditch Paranormal Research Group setting up their equipment in Room 203. Decorated in the same style as the others through the hotel, with a large original fireplace surrounded by - in what must be a health and safety nightmare - dark wooden panelling, there was no sign that the room contained any spirits other than those in the mini-bar.

The group's blind faith in the absence of any evidence baffled him. Surely if there was an afterlife one of the millions of credulous arseholes throughout history who'd ended up there would throw furniture across rooms and write tedious essays saying 'I TOLD YOU SO!' on Ouija Boards across the land. But there'd been nothing. Nada. Zip. Bugger all. Not even an ethereal out-of-office reply from beyond the grave.

Life was simple. A collection of atoms got themselves organised and nine months later you were born. You lived well (or not. The universe didn't care). Then you died. Over time, those atoms went their separate ways and got involved in the formation of another human, or a work of art, or part of the structural support of a bridge over the M62 motorway. There was no soul, no continuing consciousness, only the majesty of the human brain which had only developed the way it did because we wanted to eat tasty animals bigger than us but didn't have the fangs for the job.

While the others busied themselves with infrared cameras and motion sensors, Rick carried out his own preparations. He checked the wood-lined walls for any loose panels or secret passages and swept under the bed to look for wires or speakers. He sat on the edge of the mattress, wrinkling his nose at the horror that was the bedspread beneath him, as Lila loaded film into the back of a camera. He had to admit that she was hot, despite their idealogical differences. Cute was cute no matter how bad her life choices might be.

'Why are you using film? Isn't digital easier?' he asked her.

'It's easier to capture ghosts on film rather than digital.'

Rick rolled his eyes. *No, it's easier for mistakes to occur in the development process that can then be interpreted as ghosts*, he thought.

'The disturbances have mostly been centred on the fireplace so that's where I think we should concentrate our investigations,' Brian said with a pompous air that made Rick want to shake him by the shoulders until he came to his senses. The other three agreed with his suggestion because thinking for themselves was far too much like hard work. Rick could feel the nicotine craving scratching at the edges of his mood. He fished his e-cigarette from out of his pocket and was about to take a drag when Brian coughed politely.

'This equipment is sensitive. Can you do that outside, please?'

'I'm very sorry,' replied Rick, 'I wouldn't want to screw up your proton packs or anything.'

He gladly left them to it, slipping out of the room, heading down to the deserted reception and out into the cool night air. He vaped deeply, the atomiser burning the liquid with a satisfying crackle, and exhaled. The thick white cloud obscured the fat moon shining down on the sleeping village.

What was it they were expecting to find up there? If Rick had the luxury of eternity at his disposal, he wouldn't want to spend five minutes with that lot out of choice. He was only here because he was the newest member of the Skeptics' Society and nobody else wanted to accept the invitation to study the investigators' methods. Martin the hotelier seemed happy to have them here, even giving them a tour about the history of the building. Rick could understand why. It was all good marketing. Once word got out about their visit, he'd be able to book the rooms out to the gullible for months at a time.

Science, however, was always there to wave facts and evidence under the nose of superstition. Take the moon shining above, for example. Ancient civilisations thought it was a goddess, or made of cheese, or turned people into werewolves. Now, science proves it is simply a ball of dead rock ripped from Earth itself. The moon generates no light of its own. So, vampires couldn't exist because if one ventured out by moonlight, they'd die immediately as it reflects the sun!

'Answer me that, Brian,' Rick muttered under his breath. Still, Lunbridge seemed nice enough. There was a refreshing lack of coffee shop chains and Nandii. He let the silence wash over him. He couldn't remember the last time the world around him had been so dark and still.

Then, carried gently on the breeze, a song drifted across the fields; lilting female voices in a complex harmony. Enchanted, Rick listened to the rise and fall of the delicate melody. Probably some farm girls in the woods, drunk on cider and cavorting, which is something Rick always told himself he should do more of. Perhaps they'd enjoy the company of a sophisticated metropolitan man from the bright lights of the Midlands? He doubted the others would notice if he slipped away for a couple of hours.

Rick crossed the road, jumped the fence and headed across the dark field toward the sirens' song.

☾

Dave couldn't sleep. His eyes mapped the topography of the bed's canopy, the shadows in the fabric shifting in the breeze that blew through the open window. A myriad of questions ricocheted around his brain. What would be next for them when they returned to London? What would Death do? How much more difficult would his job be here with the paranormal investigators around? Did he put the bins out? What was going on with Tommy?

Adulthood. Confusing. Awkward. Too much admin. Wouldn't recommend to a friend. 3/10.

Still, it was better than the alternative and--

'Are you awake?' Melanie asked, a voice in the darkness.

'No,' Dave answered back. Melanie switched the bedside lamp on, bathing the bed in a pool of light and forcing Dave to cover his eyes. She rolled over onto her side to face him.

'Is it me or do things not end up well for couples in this place?'

'It doesn't have a great history for a place selling itself as a romantic hideaway.'

'I think you should deal with Ophelia and Daniel. Now. Tonight.'

Dave dropped his hands from his face and looked at Melanie as if she'd just asked him to juggle some ducks. 'What?'

She rested her head on her hands. 'If they're in that room then you need to let them cross over so they can spend eternity together. Now they have names and a story it doesn't seem right to leave them down there any longer than you have to.'

Dave reluctantly agreed with her and opened his mouth to reply when he suddenly realised that they were no longer alone. The hair on the back of his neck raised up as if the air was electrically charged. The lamp grew in luminosity until the light in the room took on a liquid quality. A dark figure, silhouetted in the glow, stood at the foot of the bed. Then, the light winked out of existence with a pop. Melanie gasped in fear. Dave reached over and turned the ceiling lights on, but the figure had vanished.

Dave had to admit that the hotel seemed to be as advertised. He could see the light in the hallway outside the room glow brighter as it seeped through the gap under the door. Throwing the covers aside, he jumped out of bed, pulled on a tatty tee shirt and, hopping around, the pyjama bottoms he'd dropped in a pile on the floor. He turned to Melanie to find she too was getting dressed.

'What are you doing?' he asked.

'You honestly expect me to stay here on my own after that little display?' she replied. Dave shrugged.

'Fair enough.' He ran across the room, took a deep breath, and opened the door.

☾

Rick wasn't a fan of nature at the best of times. There weren't enough pubs for a start, and his nocturnal walk had done nothing to improve his opinion. He continued to march grumpily, trainers caked in mud, towards the mysterious voices. He passed through a dark forest, the branches and thorns tugging at his clothes as if urging him not to continue, but he persisted. The ground developed a sharp incline and his calf muscles joined in with the chorus of complaints ringing through his skull. He stumbled, his hands and knees sinking into the wet sludge, and he let forth a string of expletives.

Never underestimate the hardship a young man will endure if cute girls might be in his near future. Rick stood up, wiped his filthy hands on the back of his jeans and continued uphill, the joyful singing getting ever louder. He imagined them all gathered around a campfire, snuggled together for warmth as they passed a bottle of something home-brewed between them.

'Hello, ladies,' he said, his most charming grin fixed to his face, as he crested the hill. Silence. The singing cut off as if a mystical finger had pressed the pause button on the universe. Confused, he took his phone from his pocket and scanned the hilltop with its flashlight. All it revealed was a set of giant standing stones arranged in a perfect circle. In the glare of the torch he could see innumerable smaller rocks set between the larger ones, each placed with equal care. He forgot about his failed seduction and walked up to a megalith as tall as he was. He ran his muddy fingers across the rough surface, wondering how long these rocks had been here. How had an early tribe dragged them up the slope and set them with such precision? What rituals were performed within the perimeter? What spirits had the monument been built to worship?

Rick looked back in the direction he'd come, surprised by the distance he'd covered. The village was a small smudge of light dabbed on the landscape. He was exhausted, his muscles knotted and heavy like wet rope. He resolved to return the following day and explore the henge further. Perhaps Lila would like to accompany him.

Rick headed back down the hill, leaning backwards to compensate for the gradient, taking stuttering steps to control his descent. Unfortunately, his foot caught a protruding rock and his body let gravity do the rest of the work as he tumbled downwards like a rag doll thrown by a short-tempered child. With a loud crunch, he came to rest in a crumpled heap.

Rick stared up at the sky, his blurred vision smearing the stars across its black canvas until they snapped back into focus and joined the correct constellations. He sat up and gingerly checked all his limbs were where they should be. An exploration of his throbbing forehead revealed a deep gash bleeding down his face. With a dirty tissue he'd found in his pocket pressed to the wound, he staggered to his feet. Now to check the real damage. As he suspected, his phone had taken the full force of the impact. The screen was shattered, the casing dented. No matter how furiously he pressed buttons or swiped the fractured glass, it refused to respond. Not even swearing helped. He shoved it back in his jeans. The fall had disorientated him and the trees obscured the village, but he limped in the direction where he thought it should be.

Soon, he entered the forest.

ℂ

If Dave had learned anything about life, it was that everybody was secretly thinking the same thing all the time. *Everyone else has it all figured out and I have no idea what I'm doing.* Sure, everyone liked to pretend they were mature adults, but it was all a front. You needed a plan. For example, after talking to Nick Broughton during that mad night a week before, it seemed good sense to have a Zombie Apocalypse Plan. The day afterwards, he'd stuck a ten-step plan to the fridge:

1. Get a shovel.
2. Read a good book now and then.
3. Eat nothing but Twiglets and Hobnobs. Society's crumbled. Treat yo' self.
4. Mistakes will happen. To err is human. To "errrrrr" is zombie.
5. If you see a child zombie. Run. They're the scariest. Fuck that shit.
6. Hit everyone you meet over the head with the shovel.
7. Hit them again.
8. Harder.

9.   Remember to floss.
10. Hit them one more time.

As he walked down the hotel corridor in fluffy slippers, Dave had no strategy other than putting one foot in front of the other and seeing what happened next. The lights above him pulsed brightly with an intense static buzz one after the other; an electromagnetic trail leading him to who knows where. He could hear the pad of Melanie's bare feet behind him, hurrying to keep up, and once again he worried that he was leading her into danger. He was no expert on relationships, but a series of life-threatening encounters with the undead was not a basis for a romance. Still, at least they were spending time together.

The trail stopped at room 203. The lights returned to the usual soft glow scientifically proven to create a relaxed mood within whoever stood beneath them. With Melanie at his shoulder, he knocked gently on the door. The lock clicked, and the door swung open, striking the wall. Inside the room, the lamps fizzed and flickered; an electrical storm contained within the four walls. Dave could see cameras and pieces of electrical equipment silhouetted against the furious bursts of light, their attention directed towards the fireplace where two figures stood; one male, one female. He was dressed in the finest velvet tailcoat and she in a delicate, ivory lace wedding dress. If they hadn't been hovering ethereally above the carpet they'd have passed for actors in a period play.

'Oh, for the love of God. Would you stop talking?' Ophelia asked, rubbing her temple with gossamer fingers. 'For two centuries I've had to listen to your banal observations. All I want is just five minutes' peace.'

'But my darling--' Daniel said.

'Can you please stop calling me that? I thought we'd agreed to just be friends.'

Dave leaned back towards Melanie. 'Can you see them?' he whispered.

'Who?' she asked.

'The Jane Austen characters arguing by the fireplace?' Melanie shook her head. 'Good.' Dave stepped into the room and cleared his throat. The ghosts looked over. He smiled awkwardly and waved. 'Sorry, am I interrupting something?'

'No, please,' Ophelia said. 'Any break from the constant whining would be a blessed relief.'

'I do not whine constantly,' Daniel whined.

Ophelia closed her eyes and took what would've been a deep breath, if she'd had any breath to take. When she opened them, she looked directly at Dave. 'Who are you, Sir? One who can commune with the dead, it seems.'

Dave moved further into the room. 'I'm Dave Marwood. I'm here to help you.'

The door of the room across the corridor opened and Brian, Lila, Griff and Jenny fell into room 203. 'What's he doing in there?' Brian yelled at Melanie, a quivering finger pointed at Dave. 'All our readings are off the charts. The infrared is picking up something we've never seen before by the fireplace. He'll ruin all our research. And what the bloody hell is going on with the electrics?'

Dave turned to Brian, a finger to his lips. 'Shhh!' he ordered. 'I'm trying to have a conversation.'

'Are you taking the piss?' Brian shouted. Melanie placed a hand on his arm, easing him back from the doorway.

'No, he's not taking the piss,' Melanie said. 'We're here for the same reason you are. Dave can, like, talk to ghosts. They're in there right now. From my experience, you'll see more than a pencil roll across a desk tonight.'

'What experience is that?' Griff asked, poking his head around the doorframe.

'Well, last week I was possessed by the fused consciousness of the souls of a suicide cult.'

'Oh,' Griff said, his gaze dropping to the floor as if hoping to find something to say laying there. 'How was that?'

'It stung a little. And, yes, Brian, UberSystems International Tower disappeared into another dimension. We're unclear on which one, though.'

'I bloody knew it,' Brian said with a self-satisfied smile.

In the room, Dave had sat down on the end of the bed. The spectral figures floated in front of the hearth, drifting around each other in a figure of eight pattern.

'Tell me, Mr Marwood. Do you have a love?' asked Ophelia.

'Yeah, my girlfriend. Her name's Melanie.' Dave pointed to the doorway. 'That's her there. Say hello, Melanie.'

Melanie, confused, waved at thin air. 'Err... Hello.'

'She does not have the gift?'

Dave shook his head. 'Nope, just me.'

Ophelia hovered close enough to make Dave nervously back up on the bed. 'And she is one who you would die for?'

'Yes,' Dave replied without thinking.

Ophelia glanced sideways at Daniel. 'Well, don't.'

'Sorry, but I thought you were star-crossed lovers or something?' Dave said, wondering if he'd walked into the wrong haunted hotel room. It happened more often than you'd think.

'We were,' Ophelia smiled sadly, 'but you really get to know someone when you're trapped together for the best part of three centuries. If I'd known he'd be this annoying, I would've let him have a fumble under my petticoats and then called it a day and married someone with a future.'

'And if I'd known you'd be so incredibly moody I wouldn't have bothered to navigate my way through those undergarments,' Daniel sniffed.

Ophelia sighed. 'It was so different when we first met. Poetry and flowers. Secret rendezvous when we would be swept up by our passions. It was so illicit and romantic. Maybe that was the problem. We were so caught up in the excitement and danger of the situation, we didn't stop to consider what would happen when the excitement had gone. I mean, it was fine at first drifting wistfully as spirits through the ether but after the first few decades all those little quirks you once found adorable became incredibly irritating.'

'How long have you been courting your lady, Mr Marwood?' asked Daniel.

Dave counted the time up on his fingers. 'About six months, on and off. We've just moved in together.'

Daniel, shocked at the immorality, placed a hand on his chest. 'And not married? My, how things have changed since our day.'

'Well, at least you can walk out the door if you can't stand the sight of one another. You won't end up with an eternity of staring at a face you can't even slap,' said Ophelia.

'Do you see what I have to put up with, Mr Marwood?' Daniel said. 'Love always dies. I thought it would last forever, but now it's just as rotten and worm-ridden as my corpse, wherever that might be buried.'

Dave felt that this kind of talk was sucking the romance out of the situation. 'Well, we're still pretty happy and, as she's watching us, it'd really help if you worked with me on this.'

'You said you can help us. How?' Daniel asked.

'I can help you move on, cross over, whatever.'

'Will there be other gentlemen there?' Ophelia asked, her interest piqued.

'I think anyone you met right now would just be a massive rebound thing. You both need time to be on your own,' Dave advised.

Daniel approached the bed. 'What do we need to do?'

Dave presented his hands, palms upwards. 'You need to put your hands in mine and the universe will sort out the rest.'

The two spirits looked at each other. 'I'm sorry, Daniel,' Ophelia said sadly. 'It's not you. It's me.' They each took one of Dave's hands. In an instant, they transformed into glowing orbs so dazzling the audience in the doorway were forced to shield their eyes. The luminescence intensified until the room was a perfect cube of light, then it was plunged into a perfectly still darkness.

After a moment, the lamps blinked and returned to their steady glow. Dave slouched on the bed, his head drooping as the others ran in. Melanie wrapped him in her arms. 'Tell me all about it. Was it romantic? Did they cry? Did they pass onto the Great Beyond hand in hand?'

Dave rested his head on her shoulder. He couldn't bring himself to tell her what had gone on. 'Something like that.'

Brian and the others were busy checking their equipment. 'Please say we got that,' Brian said to his team.

'We'll need to confirm it all back at the lab,' Jenny replied, pressing buttons on what Dave thought looked like an old reel-to-reel tape machine, 'but we've definitely recorded something.'

The others cheered, shaking hands and hugging each other, so caught up in their celebrations they didn't notice a visibly trembling Martin enter the room.

'What's going on in here? The electrics everywhere have been playing silly buggers,' he said, barely able to conceal his rage. Brian put his hands on Martin's quivering shoulders.

'It's all right, Martin. We've got them recorded.'

Martin's mood immediately brightened. 'Oh, that's marvellous. Well done, you.'

Brian turned to Dave. 'And this young man has helped them pass on to the other side. They're at peace now.'

Dave gave them a tired smile and a little wave. It was nothing.

'Oh, you little sod,' Martin spat, the anger returning.

'I beg your pardon?' asked Dave, baffled.

Martin's eyes were scanning the room. 'Yes, I can feel it now. They're not here. What have you done?' Dave opened his mouth to answer, but Martin cut him off. 'They were my USP, my unique selling point. I can't bloody well advertise a haunted hotel if I have no bloody ghosts now, can I?'

'But it was the right thing to do,' Dave replied.

'And how does that help the small businessman? Get them back!'

'I can't. That's kind of the point of the afterlife.'

Martin growled through gritted teeth, a sound made of pure anger and frustration and almost animalistic in its intensity. 'I want all this cleared up now. You've disturbed the other guests enough tonight.' He wheeled around and stormed out of the room, slamming the door behind him. Everyone looked at each other in embarrassed silence, like scolded schoolchildren. Lila wrinkled her nose up in thought.

'Does anyone know where Rick is?'

☾

Rick was lost. He was angry with himself and he was angry with the manufacturer of his phone for not building a sturdier model. He was already composing the indignant email the CEO of the company would receive when he finally got back to the hotel. But mostly he was angry with nature. It was too big, too muddy and too bloody dark. Nature was stupid. Whose idea was it anyway?

He'd blundered around, moving deeper and deeper into the woods until the canopy of leaves grew so thick they obscured the stars above. He checked the trunk of a tree because he knew moss only grew on the north side. Or was it the south? And what difference did it make anyway because he didn't know which direction the village lay?

'Help!' He called out to the treetops. A response came in the form of that same unearthly howl they'd heard in the pub garden; a cry filled with confused anguish and rage. Fear wrapped its icy fingers around Rick's throat. His heart thumped in his chest like a free-form jazz solo. The rational part of his brain told him there were no dangerous animals in this part of the country; it was just an echo, or a smaller creature's call amplified by the natural amphitheatre of the terrain. Another, more primitive part screamed that an unspeakable, demon-eyed monster was coming to devour him and that he should run for his life. The second part won the argument and Rick turned and sprinted away from the direction of the noise. He stumbled over fallen branches, kicking up mulch and leaves, the trees' limbs slashing at his face and arms, but the adrenaline flooding his system numbed the pain.

A twig snapped as loud as a firecracker in the stillness of the night. Rick could hear the raking of branches behind him, the regulated pattern of four feet pounding the floor, the panting of a large creature. He was filled with the fear that came with the knowledge that the ancient ritual of predator and prey was being played out. He didn't dare look behind him, but he had an impression of the great strength and weight of the creature by the crunch and tear of foliage as it charged through the undergrowth.

Tears streaming down his face, Rick tried to call out, but his breath caught in his throat, choking him. Then, through a gap in the trees, he glimpsed a light. He'd muddled his way back to civilisation. He almost laughed at his good fortune. Whatever was chasing him was a wild animal and would fear man - inventor of fire and electricity and dominator of the natural world. If Rick could make it to the edge of the village, he was sure he would be safe. He just had to keep the distance between them for a few more seconds. He found another kick of speed and vaulted a fallen spruce tree, filled with the confidence of man's superiority over wild animals. His trainers clipped the broken nub of a branch stump and he landed awkwardly, his legs jarring up into his body. He ground his teeth and pushed through the pain travelling up his spine.

That stumble had allowed the creature to gain ground and with a final leap, it dug four sets of claws into Rick's back. They crashed to the ground, the momentum sending them sliding through the leaves, filling Rick's mouth and nose with dirt. The talons raked across his back, carving valleys of ripped flesh that immediately flooded with rivers of blood. His face pressed to the forest floor, Rick's screams were muffled by the mud. He struggled to free himself; pinned down by the superior strength of the animal. He could smell the rotten stench of a carnivore's breath and feel the thick, black, greasy fur brush against his cold skin. He sobbed, tears mixing with the dirt, senselessly begging this feral, indifferent beast for mercy, until a powerful set of jaws silenced him with a swift snap of the neck.

The moon, the only witness to the horror, slipped behind a cloud.

SATURDAY

'Toast is brilliant. Whoever thought, "This bread we've already cooked, yeah? I reckon we should try cooking it again." was a genius,' Dave said as he spread butter thickly over the slice on the plate in front of him. Melanie watched him from the other side of the breakfast table with a kind of amused puzzlement. Just a few hours ago, this man was talking with centuries-old spirits. That would be enough to shake even the hardiest of souls.

Melanie had never seen Dave carry out the work he was paid for until the previous night and the way he had treated the dead with dignity and respect made it hard to believe this was the same boy who'd insulted twelve-year-olds' mums when they beat him playing online video games. Melanie loved Dave, she was sure of that, but now she felt something else. *I'm proud of you*, she thought. Perhaps coming here *had* been a good idea.

Dave noticed the faint smile on Melanie's lips. 'What's up? Have I got something on my face?'

'Nothing,' she replied with a smile. 'Just basking in your boyish charm.'

'Damn straight,' Dave said, licking his butter-smeared fingers.

It was a beautiful morning, the sun spilling into the dining room from a crisp blue sky. Melanie was bathed in a shaft of warm light that seemed to recharge her tired body. It occurred to her that if Dave hadn't saved her from the massacre in UberSystems International Tower, this simple act would have reduced her to a pile of ashes.

'What do you want to do today?' she asked, conscious not to dwell on such thoughts. Dave shrugged.

'Whatever you want to do. I'm just happy to do it with you.'

As if by magic, Martin appeared at their table. 'Sir. Madam.' A small nod, his forehead creased into a frown, his hands clasped in a display of contrition. 'I'd like to apologise for my behaviour last night. It was inexcusable. As a way of making amends, we'd be delighted if you would dine with us this evening as our guests, at no charge to yourselves.' Dave and Melanie exchanged glances.

'Thank you very much. That'd be delightful,' Dave replied. His body was rigid, his language formal, as it always was when he was talking to someone he wasn't close to.

'Excellent. Thank you for your understanding. Just so we're clear, there are, of course, no such things as ghosts or spirits and a man as worldly wise as yourself could see that what we do here is nothing more than tongue-in-cheek marketing.'

Dave nodded. 'Of course.'

Martin's demeanour immediately changed from penitent to charming host. 'Marvellous. Now, what may I get you for breakfast?'

Once they'd given their orders, including more toast, Martin headed back to the kitchen, stopping to rearrange the cutlery on an unoccupied table with brisk efficiency. Melanie leaned across the table.

'That was odd,' she said in a hushed tone.

'I know. I can't believe they'd run out of grilled tomatoes.'

Melanie shook her head. 'No, I mean, last night he was all ready to throw us out onto the streets because we were destroying his business model and now he's telling us he's made it all up.'

Dave shrugged. 'Hey, as long as I'm getting a free steak out of it, he can tell me anything he wants.'

It was now Brian's turn to arrive at their table, a worried look on his face. 'Have you seen Rick this morning?' Dave and Melanie both shook their heads. 'We can't find him anywhere and his bed hasn't been slept in.'

'Maybe he's gone home?' Dave suggested. 'He seemed pretty annoyed by you lot.'

'I don't know how. We all came in the minibus together. Nobody amongst the staff ordered him a taxi, or even talked to him.'

'When was the last time anybody saw him?' asked Melanie.

'He was with us and then went outside before you showed up. We're organising a search party.'

'We'd be glad to help if you need us,' Melanie replied.

'Thank you. We're meeting outside in half an hour.' Brian hurried off, wringing his hands tightly, concerned about his errant student. Dave sat back in his chair.

'I know I say this about a lot of places we go to, but this place is weird.'

☾

Melanie and Dave were standing on the hill over-looking Lunbridge. When the search party had been dividing up the workload back at the hotel, Melanie had suggested they look for Rick up here. Even if they didn't find him, maybe they could use it as a vantage point to coordinate the search, but there was no sign of him on the hilltop or down below. She had to admit that her suggestion had been partly selfish, as she'd wanted to visit the standing stones since reading about them on the hotel website. The light up here was so sharp it took her breath away. It was if the city was filtered through an old, grey cathode-ray tube, but out here the resolution of the world had been turned up to Ultra High Definition. The colours were so intense that she squinted for fear of damaging her eyes as she looked over the fields and hills rolling over the horizon.

Dave meandered between the giant stones as if hypnotised by them, taking care not to step on the smaller rocks scattered around. 'How long do you think these have been here?' he asked, his voice hushed with wonder. Melanie took a guidebook from the small rucksack on her back and thumbed through the pages until she came to the relevant section.

"'Legend tells that the stones were originally a coven of witches, petrified by the evil Lord Michael of Lunbridge after they placed a spell on his daughter, turning her into a wolf. It was proclaimed that Gwyneth Frost and her daughters had profaned the Sabbath by dancing upon the hilltop overlooking the village and so were turned to stone as punishment.'"

Dave snatched his hand away from the rock and wiped it on his jeans. 'Oh no, I might've been touching a witch's boob.'

Melanie gazed up from the book to shoot a disappointed look in his direction before continuing to read aloud. "'Many say the stone circle is imbued with magic and often, late at night, the witches can be heard singing. Only those truly in love will be able to count the same number of stones twice. If they are successful, legend says the spell will be broken, and the witches released.'"

'Really?' said Dave. 'That sounds like a challenge.' He turned and started to count the rocks.

'Don't do that,' Melanie called out to him.

'Why not?'

'Isn't it going to be awkward when you count them all and nothing happens?'

Dave smiled. 'You're such a cynic. After all you've seen, you don't believe there can't be a little magic in this world?'

Melanie opened her mouth to answer when a high-pitched scream sliced through the air. Melanie and Dave looked at each other. They'd heard that kind of scream before.

Rick had been found.

☾

Melanie and Dave sprinted back down the hill, their feet almost flying out from under them. They barrelled into the forest toward the screams, the branches whipping them so ferociously they were forced to shield their faces with their bare arms. By the time they'd reached the source of the commotion, a large crowd made up of hotel staff and villagers had gathered around what remained of Rick.

Melanie's stomach turned. Whatever had attacked him had done so with such ferocity she only recognised him from the tee shirt he'd been wearing the previous night, now torn to shreds. She'd seen horrors before, but even the aftermath of a vampire assault couldn't come close to the animal savagery in front of her. The leaves and grass beneath the body were soaked with pools of blood running out in thick rivers from deep wounds carved into the skin. It was as if something had tried to rip out his soul. She turned away when she saw his hollowed-out stomach, ashamed that she felt glad when someone covered him with a blanket.

Martin soon arrived to take charge of the situation. 'Everybody back!' he shouted, trampling an invisible barrier around the body that the onlookers instinctively retreated from. 'I've called the emergency services and they're on their way. Please, give this young man some dignity.'

Dave seemed dazed, staring off into the forest, so Melanie held his hand and led him back. His reaction was understandable. Murder and madness seemed to follow him wherever he went these days. Could he be worried that he, and his powers, were responsible for this? Still, Death would have been here and seen what had happened. He would know she and Dave were in the area and would make everything okay.

The police soon arrived along with two paramedics, though it was too late for their skills. They quickly cordoned off the area with yellow tape and ordered everyone back to the hotel to begin their enquiries. As they walked back across the fields, Melanie took Dave by the hand.

'Are you all right?' she asked quietly, a supportive smile on her lips. Dave continued to stare at the ground just in front of him.

'Rick. He was still there, on the edge of the clearing,' he replied, his words heavy with disappointment. 'Death didn't come for him.'

☾

Rick's body was gathered up, placed carefully in thick black plastic bags and carried away in the back of the ambulance while the police took photographs of the remains of the feeding frenzy. They then extensively questioned anyone that had interacted with Rick the previous day. When had they seen him last? Had he been drinking? Was he acting strangely?

'Is this all necessary?' Dave asked the two uniformed officers who'd set up a makeshift interview room in the inn's saloon bar. He was keen to get back out there and find out what had happened to Rick. 'It was obviously an animal attack.'

The taller officer straightened his tunic. 'That's what it looks like, but seeing as the largest animal anyone's seen in that forest is a slightly irritable badger the locals named Angry Keith, we need to establish a timeline of Mr Cartwright's movements for the coroner's report.'

'We may be dealing with an escaped dangerous animal,' continued the shorter officer, who'd never seen a dead body in the line of duty until today. He was already thinking how the way that he had handled this case would be great evidence for his next appraisal, so long as nobody mentioned the vomiting.

It was late by the time the questioning had finished and Martin insisted that the Paranormal Investigation Group had a drink on the house before they made their way back home. Dave watched them from the other side of the bar; a solemn mourning party for the late Richard Cartwright.

'Perhaps we should go too,' Melanie said. 'The police have our details if they need to get in touch.'

'Hmmm,' he replied, the noise non-committal. Dave didn't know where Death was, or what he was up to. He'd texted both him and Anne, but there'd been no reply. All he knew was that Rick was out there, alone and confused. He was so close to the living, calling out to them, the words disappearing into the void between. Dave understood that loneliness; the knowledge that life had so callously thrown him aside. He couldn't sit here in the warmth of the bar while Rick was abandoned in the cold he could no longer feel. Also, he'd been promised a free steak.

'He should never have been out there,' one of the regulars slurred. He'd propped himself up on the bar since they'd found Rick's body. His weather-worn face was ruddy with drink and he'd reached the stage of inebriation where it was important that everybody knew his opinions and agreed that they were correct. 'This is what happens when you invite strangers in.'

'Now, Jack,' Martin said. 'There's no need for talk like that.'

Jack pushed his flat cap back and waved a gnarled finger under Martin's nose. 'I told you this would come and bite you in the arse.' He turned to face the room. 'It'll come and bite you all in the arse.'

In the corner, Lila sobbed quietly. Martin walked around to the other side of the bar and took Jack by the arm. 'Maybe it's time for you to sleep this off. It's been a trying day for everyone.' Jack seemed to deflate at Martin's touch, submitting to the landlord's authority.

'Aye, you're right,' he muttered. He lurched towards the door and, clumsily doffing his cap, disappeared into the night. Martin turned to the table where Brian and the others sat.

'I'm very sorry about that. Jack finds this sort of thing hard to deal with.'

Dave shifted in his seat to face Martin. 'Does this sort of thing happen a lot, then?'

Martin laughed nervously. 'Of course not. Nothing of consequence happens in Lunbridge.' He hurried back behind the bar and busied himself with stocking the shelves. Dave turned to Melanie.

'I'm sorry, but I don't think we can leave just yet. I need to do this, I can't leave him out there,' Dave said as much to himself as to Melanie. She sighed, knowing he was right.

'Well, I suppose we'd better get it over with.' They stood up and headed for the door. As they brushed past Brian's table, he reached out and grabbed Dave by the arm, his eyes not moving from the half-empty glass in front of him.

'Is Rick all right?'

Dave tried on his most confident smile. 'Yes, he's moved on.'

'Just shut up,' Jenny spat. 'I don't know what kind of light show you pulled off last night, or why you did it, but this is sick.'

Dave looked at her, steely-eyed and sure. 'It doesn't matter what you think.'

Brian nodded. 'Thank you, Dave. He was my responsibility, and I let him down. It's good he's at peace, at least.'

'You don't actually believe him, do you?' Jenny asked with incredulity.

'You saw it as well as I did. You reviewed the footage. Something happened in that room last night. This young man has a gift and nobody sat at this table can deny it.'

Happy he'd put Brian's mind at rest, if just for a moment, Dave said, 'Have a safe journey home everyone.'

'Goodbye,' said Melanie, and four sad smiles were the reply. She and Dave continued towards the exit when Martin cleared his throat.

'I hope you're not thinking about going out there tonight.'

Dave turned around. 'We just wanted to get a bit of fresh air.'

Martin waved a hand and Dave heard the regulars' barstools scraping on the stone floor as they stood up. 'I'd suggest you wait until morning for that. Your safety is my only concern.'

Not wanting a confrontation, Dave smiled. 'Of course, you're right. We should get ready for dinner, anyway.'

'That sounds like an excellent idea,' Martin replied.

☾

Dave and Melanie listened to the rumble of the university minibus driving out of the village and the last of the regulars stumbling back to their homes. Dave paced across the bedroom floor, while Melanie perched on the edge of the bed, her feet tapping, a bundle of nervous energy, a flash of something silver in her hands.

'What's that?' Dave asked. Melanie showed him a silver letter opener.

'It was the only sharp object I could find.'

'There's never a flaming sword around when you need one,' Dave muttered to himself. 'I don't think I'll need that. He's on the edge of the forest. I need to go in, sort him out, and come back again.' He walked over to Melanie and knelt before her, taking her hands in his. 'It'll take about five minutes, tops.'

'I'm coming with you.'

'No, you're not.'

'We're in this together. You need someone to watch your back.'

'Yeah, but--'

Melanie spun the letter opener in her palm. 'I'm a strong, independent woman who's more than capable of slaying wild animals, vampires or any other creature stalking the night.'

'You're right,' Dave replied, chastised. 'Let's do this.' He kissed her and, to display a confidence he wasn't feeling, tried to strut over to the window. As Dave wasn't built to strut, his foot caught on the edge of a rug and he staggered the rest of the way across the room. He turned back to a concerned Melanie. 'Really, we'll be fine.'

Dave pushed the window open and let the cool breeze caress his face. He climbed out onto the ledge and, looking down into the darkness, let himself drop onto the flat roof below, landing gently, perfectly balanced, as graceful as a cat. He looked up to an empty window.

'Of course she doesn't see *that*,' he whispered to himself. Melanie's head finally appeared, her hair pulled up into a ponytail. She was all business. Dave signalled for her to follow him. He dangled himself over the edge of the building and, half-falling, half-climbing, clambered down the drainpipe until he reached the lawn. Melanie slid effortlessly down after him.

They skirted the edges of the property in a crouched run, keeping to the shadows, until they reached a low stone wall. They scrambled over, scraping elbows and scuffing up clothing. Once they were on the other side, they knew they were out of sight of anyone who might gaze out of one of the hotel's windows. Melanie flicked on the torchlight on her phone and they followed its beam towards the tree line, the long grass swishing past their legs with a hypnotic rhythm. Dave looked up into the black sky etched with a thousand constellations unfamiliar to him since his time in the city. Here, stripped of the trappings of the twenty-first century, he and Melanie did not differ from the animals that inhabited the woods. He felt at peace, until the hoot of an owl reminded him that there were hunters among the trees. He told himself that David Attenborough had once said big cats only hunt every two to five days. And Attenborough hadn't let him down before.

Soon, they arrived at the clearing where they had found Rick's body. The blue and white police tape, strung in-between four trees, fluttered in the wind. The moon appeared from behind the clouds, coating the scene in an extra layer of creepiness. Dave ducked beneath the ribbon and stopped in his tracks.

'I think I stepped in some Rick,' he said, checking the bottom of his shoe. While he was busy wiping the sole on a bed of dry leaves, a figure stepped out from behind a tree. The torchlight shone through his torso as if he wasn't there. Which was true, depending on what plane of existence you were observing reality from.

'Dave?' the figure asked in a quiet, scared voice. Dave stopped cleaning his shoes. It seemed like the polite thing to do.

'Hello, Rick.'

'You can see me?' Rick smiled sheepishly. 'Well, this is embarrassing.'

'Yeah, there are probably easier ways to discover your entire outlook on life was wrong.'

'And you can talk to the dead?'

'Pretty much.'

'So, there's an afterlife?'

'Dude, there's an afterlife, a Grim Reaper, other dimensions, the lot.'

'And God?'

Dave shrugged. 'The jury's still out on that one.'

Rick looked disappointed. 'Oh. I had a bunch of questions I wanted to ask him.'

'Haven't we all? You've changed your tune.'

'Yeah, well, dying really helps to change your perspective. I've had a lot of time to think.'

'What happened?' Dave asked. 'What were you even doing out here?'

Rick sighed. 'I thought I heard some girls party-ing and came out to have a look, but I was wrong. What there was, though, was a great big bloody wolf that ate me. Do you know what it's like to watch yourself get torn apart by a wild animal?' Rick waved the question away. 'Of course not. Sorry. That's a stupid thing to ask.'

'A wolf?' Dave asked Rick. 'Are you sure?'

'Big, black furry thing with massive teeth? Howls at the moon? I know what a wolf looks like.'

'The Beast of Lunbridge,' Dave whispered to him-self.

'So, since then I've just been out here on my own. You all turned up, but nobody could see or hear me. God, death is so depressing. Is this it? It seems dull. I don't even get to go bump in the night,' Rick said, his hand passing right through a trunk of a tree as if it wasn't there. Or as if he wasn't there. Again, planes of reality. 'There's a whole list of people I want to get haunting, starting with several ex-girlfriends.'

Dave looked at his watch. 'I'm not sure that's how it works.'

Melanie looked behind her. She gripped the letter opener tucked into her belt. 'Something's out there.' Dave thought he heard a twig snap. His muscles tensed, his entire body straining to take flight. Rick had noticed it too.

'You'd better get out of here,' he said. Melanie was already backing away towards the cover of the tree line, treading carefully around the fallen branches. Dave moved in the opposite direction, to-wards Rick.

'This is goodbye, then,' Dave said, holding his hand out.

Rick looked at Dave's open hand. 'You're just going to leave me here?'

Dave shook his head. 'No, it's time for you to move on. Take my hand.'

Rick smiled. 'The start of a big adventure.'

'Something like that.'

'Good to meet you, Dave.'

'You too, Rick.' Rick grabbed Dave's hand and, after a flash of light that illuminated the trees as if day had gatecrashed the night, he was gone.

'What did he say did it?' Melanie asked as they made their way out of the clearing.

'A wolf,' Dave whispered in reply.

'A wolf? This far south?'

Dave shrugged. 'That's what he told me.'

'What do they say you should do if a wolf attacks?' Melanie asked. 'Make yourself big?'

'That's bears,' said Dave, shaking his head.

'How about bright lights?'

'That's Mogwai. I think you're meant to stand your ground, stay together, safety in numbers, shout at it. Don't turn your back.' A deep growl rumbled out from the undergrowth; a throaty snarl that turned Dave's bowels to water. He swallowed hard. 'Sod that. Leg it.'

Melanie turned on her heels and sprinted away. Dave ran after her and had soon caught up. Something large and powerful burst out from its hiding place behind them, crashing through the thick vegetation, hunting them down. Dave and Melanie scrambled up the overgrown bank, their feet slipping on the slick grass, and made it onto the road leading back to the hotel. The creature followed them, the pounding of paws on the tarmac growing louder as it ate up the distance. Dave was hoping that distance would be the only thing it would eat this evening when he was suddenly pulled to the ground. The animal was solid and powerful, its fur so black the moonlight seemed to fall into it. Dave tried to wrestle with the wolf, but it pinned him to the tarmac. Teeth snapped away in powerful jaws, searching for something to latch onto, but Dave's quick reactions stopped them getting any purchase on his soft flesh.

He wasn't quick enough, though, and soon it found Dave's shoulder. Dave screamed as hot needles of pain buried themselves under his skin. Instinctively, he lashed out with his fists, connecting with the wolf's head until it released him and the unbearable pressure on his bones subsided. His left arm limp and useless, Dave dragged himself away. Then the hot, sour breath of the wolf was on his neck and Dave closed his eyes, resigned to the inevitable. The searing pain had scattered his thoughts, but he knew that when he saw Death again, he would have a massive go at him.

Instead of the fury of tearing flesh he expected, there was a wet thump and a heavy weight falling on his chest. He opened his eyes to see Melanie desperately plunging the silver letter opener again and again into the wolf's side. Dark blood pumped from the wound, matting the wolf's coat of hair and running down her arm. The creature's howl of pain petered out to a frightened whimper. Throwing itself off Dave, it staggered drunkenly until its legs gave way. It collapsed onto the black ribbon of the road, the letter opener buried deep in its flesh, nothing more than a bag of bones now.

'So, who's saved the other's life more times now?' Melanie asked, bloody hands on her hip.

'I've lost count,' Dave replied, a crack in his voice. Now she'd had her moment, Melanie bent over, shaky hands on quivering legs. She looked over at where the wolf had fallen and her expression darkened. Something was wrong.

'No-no-no!' she yammered. *What now?* Dave thought, suddenly exhausted. He lazily turned his head to the side. Instead of the hairy black corpse of a wild animal something soft, pink and all-too-human was curled up in the middle of the road. A wiry young man. The letter opener was plunged deep into his heart, pointing towards Melanie like an accusing finger.

'Of course,' Dave muttered to himself before his body decided that staying conscious was overrated. Everything went black.

SUNDAY

Dave dreamt of a blood moon. Heavy and red, it swung above him like a pendulum in the sky, as if some universal clock was counting down his time in this world. He ran through a forest, surefooted across the uneven terrain, on the hunt. He couldn't see his prey, but he knew it was out there, cowering among the trees, and the knowledge he was feared gave him strength. His shoulder still ached, and tendrils of pain coursed through his body, but with that pain was a power he'd never experienced before. The wind gusted through the leaves and the trees sang to him in whispers. He stopped his run, dropped to a crouch, and stepped carefully through the long grass. He sensed his prey's heartbeat skittering and skipping arrhythmically and it filled him with joy, heat spreading through his belly as he drew nearer. Soon, he came to a clearing spotlit by the killing moon.

There she was: Melanie. She turned in a slow circle, her eyes darting to the shadows, knowing she was being stalked, but unaware of where the attack would come from. Dave imagined how easy it would be to snap her delicate bones. The stench of fear hung thick in the air and that excited him. He waited. He was a patient creature.

She turned her back to him and that was when he pounced. Running from out of the tree line, he bounded across the glade and leapt, his hands bent into claws and--

Dave jerked awake, the graceful body of his dreams replaced by an aching sack of bones. The world snapped back into focus and he processed each sensation as it returned to him. His joints seemed to have been riveted together with bolts of white-hot metal. It was daylight and he was in a bed, the cotton sheets cooling his burning flesh. He heard a noise; a cry of pain. His hand wrapped tightly around something. His gaze followed his arm, and he saw he had grabbed somebody's wrist, his nails sinking into the thick tweed of a jacket, a stranger's face wincing back at him.

Dave released his grip. 'Sorry,' he muttered through cracked, dry lips. 'Bad dream. Who are you? Where am I? Where's Melanie?'

The tweedy man gave him a professional smile. 'I'm Doctor Wilson, you're in your hotel room and Melanie is asleep next door. She hadn't left your side since we brought you here. I had to be most insistent she got some rest.'

The pain had tightened in Dave's left shoulder and he gingerly touched it, a heavy bandage beneath his fingers. 'Why aren't I in the hospital?'

'It's too far away, and you were in no condition to travel. If you hadn't received immediate medical treatment, you wouldn't be here now.'

'So now I'm stabilised, you'll be moving me?'

'Well, there may be some complications.' The doctor's eyes flickered towards the corner of the room as if seeking approval and Dave realised they weren't alone.

'Complications?' Dave repeated, confused.

'Perhaps you and Melanie should hear this together,' Dr Wilson said. 'I'll just pop next door and get her.' He retreated from the room and when the door shut, Dave lifted his head from the pillow. It felt as heavy as a bowling ball. He could see an old man he recognised from the pub the night before, sat stiffly in an armchair.

'Jack, isn't it?' Dave asked. The old man nodded. 'What are you doing here?'

Jack gave a sad sigh, the air rattling around his lungs. 'You killed Tommy last night. You killed my older brother. I told you things would come and bite you in the arse.'

☾

Melanie peered through the heavy curtains framing the hotel room window, looking down on the road that ran past the Half Moon Inn. The tarmac was scrubbed clean of the violence that had taken place the night before. No evidence remained that she'd plunged a blade into a living creature that had died a man. When dawn broke, a thin plume of smoke rose from behind the church, splitting the blushed sky. A hastily organised cremation, Melanie assumed.

This wasn't how she'd imagined her life would turn out. This wasn't part of the plan. She'd had it all mapped out. University. Then a job in the city. Her twenties would be spent doing adventurous things and meeting interesting people. Management role by thirty. Perhaps a passionate affair with a handsome billionaire if she had the time. On the company board by her mid-thirties and then a husband with a good beard, a move to the countryside and children.

She wondered if her life had become a little *too* adventurous and the people she'd met were a little *too* interesting. It would be easier to walk away, but that wasn't an option now, not after everything she'd seen. She couldn't return to a normal life knowing this world existed. She was forever bonded with Dave. If she'd been told the skinny guy with unmanageable hair, who'd deleted the TPR spreadsheet by the afternoon of his first day at UberSystems International, would be the bravest person she'd ever meet, she would've laughed. No matter what happened from now on, he was the love of her life and she believed she was his. The question was, how long would their lives even be at this rate?

She'd tried to sleep, but whenever she'd closed her eyes all she'd seen was Tommy's fear staring out of the darkness. After he died, her priority was to not let Dave suffer the same fate. Remembering a day's first aid training from some years earlier, she'd taken her jacket off and pressed it down on his wounds to staunch the bleeding. When it was obvious this wouldn't be good enough, she'd made the difficult decision to leave him and head back to the hotel for help.

Covered in scratches, blood and filth, she'd brought the conversation and laughter to a sudden halt when she burst into the bar.

'Help!' Melanie yelled, teetering on the brink of hysteria. Martin looked at her blood-encrusted clothes and knew what had happened. He put down the glass he'd been polishing with a greying rag, walked around the side of the bar and took charge of the situation.

'Billy, get Dr Wilson,' he barked to a drinker perched on a barstool then, to Melanie, 'Show me where they are.'

They ran into the night, leading a procession of pub regulars to where the two bodies were stretched lifelessly across the road. They looked so delicate, Melanie thought, with their limbs bent across the tarmac. Like birds struck by a speeding car. Martin crouched down and gently turned Tommy's face up to his own. Dead eyes stared glassily skywards as Martin muttered, 'Oh, Tommy. What have you done now?'

Dr Wilson arrived soon after them, a leather medical case in his hand, and worked on Dave's injuries. Melanie stood over him, watching his hands move expertly as he patched and repaired the damaged flesh.

'It was a wolf,' she tried to explain to anyone who'd listen, the words tumbling over each other. 'I swear. He attacked us.'

'Let's get him back to the hotel,' Dr Wilson said, ignoring Melanie as if she'd been mentioning the weather. Some villagers picked Dave up and, under the doctor's instructions, carried him down the road while the others gathered around Tommy's fallen body.

They carried Dave all the way to his hotel room and, once he was laid out on the bed, Melanie saw for the first time the bloody gash that ran in a semi-circle around his shoulder; a bite mark larger than any human could inflict. The doctor cleaned and stitched the wound and wrapped it delicately in gauze and bandages until he'd done all he could. Now, they had to wait.

Melanie had stayed at Dave's bedside throughout the night until she'd nodded off. Martin had stood her up and tenderly guided her into the room next door. When he'd put her to bed, he'd unplugged the telephone, tucked it under his arm and left her alone, locking the room's door from the outside. Melanie had been too exhausted to question his actions. When she realised sleep had only been teasing her, she took a shower, scrubbing away the blood that streaked her body; letting the cold water carry it away.

It was only when she went to dress herself that she realised she'd left her phone in the other room. She'd banged on the door and called out, but soon realised that nobody would come. They'd shut her away and taken all means of communicating to the outside world. They didn't want her to escape, and she didn't want to either: not without Dave, and not until her questions had been answered.

So, there she sat, on the edge of the bed, watching the full moon set over the village as its shift ended and the sun eagerly came on duty.

A full moon. A man who turned into a wolf and back again. The bite marks on Dave's body. She ran these thoughts around and around until sleep finally pulled her to its chest.

☾

Jack stared at Dave. He'd said nothing since telling Dave that Tommy was dead; just passed a bloodied letter opener from one hand to the other. At first Dave thought it was a dramatic pause, but the silence continued and now it had just become awkward. To be honest, Dave wasn't sure he'd want to hear the answers to questions he might ask. To his relief, the door opened and Dr Wilson led Melanie in. She ran over and hugged Dave tightly. He groaned as her weight pushed against his tender ribs and, embarrassed, she let him go again so he banged his head against the headboard.

'Good to have you back again,' Dave said as he rubbed his scalp.

'Sorry. I'm just glad you're all right,' Melanie replied, her eyes wet with tears.

There was a knock on the door and Martin poked his head around. 'Have you started without me?'

'No, you're just in time,' Dr Wilson replied, mirroring Martin's serious tone.

'Ah. Good,' Martin said and invited himself in. Dave noticed he was clutching a carrier bag, and he stood at the foot of the bed next to Dr Wilson. Dave shifted along the mattress to allow Melanie to perch next to him.

'What's going on?' she asked.

'What do you remember about last night, Dave?' Dr Wilson asked.

Dave's memories were sketchy, with holes carved out by sharp claws. He shrugged. 'Not much. We went into the woods.'

'Why would you do that?' Martin asked, the frustration in his voice palpable.

Dave and Melanie exchanged glances. 'We thought we left something behind,' she said.

'Couldn't it have waited until the morning?'

Dave shook his head. 'No.'

'What else?' Dr Wilson asked.

'Something attacked us. The animal that killed Rick. Tommy was the Beast of Lunbridge.'

Jack placed the letter opener on the desk. 'The Beast of Lunbridge? That's just a myth,' he spat. 'Tommy was a good boy, if a little boisterous and impetuous. He loved to run through the forest on a moonlit night. I told him it was unwise with so many strangers around, but the lad rarely listened.'

'Then you killed him,' Martin said with an accusing glare.

'No, he didn't,' Melanie said.

'We found him there next to the body!' Martin said.

'I did it.'

89

The other three stared at her, dumbfounded. 'Oh, we assumed--'

Melanie rolled her eyes. 'Of course you did.' She decided now would not be the time to debate sexism in the supernatural community.

Dave understood what was going on. 'Is there a pamphlet I could read, or anything?' he asked Dr Wilson. 'Something with the title "So, You've Been Bitten by a Werewolf"?'

'Do you have any questions? We can try to answer them.' Dr Wilson replied.

'Do you think a giant battle station exploding in orbit around the Endor would've destroyed the atmosphere and doomed the Ewoks?'

Martin pinched the bridge of his nose and squeezed his eyes shut tightly. He felt one of his headaches coming on. 'About this.'

'Oh. No then,' Dave said, shaking his head. Martin looked at him quizzically.

'Why aren't you more worried?'

'This isn't my first rodeo, Martin. And, I'll be honest with you,' Dave said, easing back into the pillow. 'It's been a tough week. I came here to relax and I'm doing all I can to keep that vibe going.'

'But Dave will be all right, won't he? If the werewolf that bit him is dead, doesn't that stop the curse or something?' asked Melanie.

'Not everything you see in the movies is true,' explained Martin. 'It doesn't work for every evil undead tribe. Vampires, yes. Conservative party members, yes. Not werewolves.'

'What's the cure, then?'

Dr Wilson sighed. 'There isn't one. By the time the moon rises tonight, Dave will become a savage beast. When he kills for the first time, his soul will be trapped forever in torment.'

'Well, it's not all bad,' said Dave with forced jollity. 'I've always wanted to be immortal and be able to grow a beard and you always said you wanted a pet.'

'You wouldn't be immortal, though you will age at a much slower rate than a normal human,' Jack chimed in. 'Oh, and the loved ones are usually the first to be slaughtered.'

'You seemed to have done fine,' Dave said.

'I was staying with family the first time Tommy turned. I was lucky. Our parents less so. We were prepared the next month.'

'If you knew that would happen, why did you let so many people stay here on a full moon?' Melanie asked.

Martin shrugged. 'I needed the money. Do you know how hard it is in the tourism business? And you've not helped me out getting rid of the ghosts.'

'All I know is that the Half Moon Inn will be getting a terrible review on Trip Advisor,' Melanie grumbled.

'I didn't think people'd go wandering around the bloody place!'

'Over the years Tommy had got better at controlling it,' Jack said. 'Sure, the odd sheep got a bit of a chewing, but he was all right. We all made sure of that.'

'I'm sure if we could contact the authorities, we can sort all this unfortunate business out,' Melanie said, the voice of reason.

'When one of our own is hurt, we sort it out amongst ourselves,' Martin replied.

'So, how are you going to sort it out?' Dave asked.

Martin reached into the plastic bag and pulled out an unopened bottle of whisky.

'Drinking competition?' Dave asked hopefully. Dr Wilson reached into his medical bag and produced a brown plastic bottle. He shook the contents.

'Sleeping pills,' he said.

'If we must, we will kill you, but we'd rather you did it yourself, on your own terms,' Martin explained.

'Can I order room service?' Dave asked. 'A sandwich? A packet of crisps? You could put some poison in it. Call it a 'suicide packed' lunch.'

Martin ignored Dave's joke. 'We can't let you leave here. It would be too dangerous.' Dave nodded. He understood. Melanie gasped.

'I've been bitten by a werewolf, Melanie,' Dave sighed. 'We both know what I have to do. I can't roam the moors for centuries. I'm not the outdoor type.' Melanie nodded, wiping her eyes. She looked skywards, breathing deeply, trying to control the tears. Dave imagined happily tearing out her exposed throat. Horrified, he shook the image from his head.

Martin nodded, glad they were all in agreement. 'You have until sunset.'

They left the ingredients for Dave's final cocktail on the desk, next to the bloody silver letter opener, and left Melanie and Dave on their own.

☾

'You're not actually going to go through with it, are you?' Melanie asked as soon as she heard the click of the door's lock.

Dave looked at her as if she was mad. 'Of course I'm bloody not. We're going to escape.' He gritted his teeth and pulled himself up, swinging his legs out of the bed. His bones were on fire and his head swam, but he brushed away Melanie's attempts to help him. 'No, I need to do this myself.'

He made his way to the wardrobe; tiny, delicate steps as if he didn't want to wake the beast sleeping inside him. With a small smile, he pulled out the Hawaiian shirt. He held it out to Melanie. 'A little help, please?'

Melanie's face wrinkled up in disgust. 'Don't make me do it.'

'It's the only item of clothing I've got left.'

Melanie sighed and snatched it from his hand. She eased one of his arms through a sleeve and then the other, making sure the material didn't catch on the thick swathes of bandages.

'I don't suppose they left our phones behind?' Dave asked as Melanie clumsily buttoned up his shirt. Her fingers were shaking, her fear filling his nostrils. He licked his lips before taking her hands in his.

'Don't worry. We'll get out of this. We always have before.'

'Have you got a plan?'

Dave shrugged. 'It's more a high-level proposition. How long have we got until sunset?' Melanie looked at her watch.

'Five hours?'

'If we can get to the car, we can make it back to London.'

Melanie folder her arms. 'Are you sure you want to head into a densely populated area?'

'Maybe Death or Anne will know what to do. Let's try to find a phone and call them, at least.' Dave hobbled over to the window and peered through the curtains. He saw Carter, the ageing bellboy, and one of the pub's regulars milling around the car park, cutting off an escape route.

The fact that he was getting used to this kind of situation unnerved Dave. His heart pumped in his chest, flooding his system with adrenaline. His thoughts pinballed as he calculated the variables. He was strangely excited. This is what it felt like to be alive. He intended to keep that going for as long as possible.

But what if they couldn't find a cure? What would happen when the moon rose? He had to admit, he was curious. Until now, he'd been a tourist in a strange and foreign land, an onlooker peering over the wall dividing the natural and supernatural. Here was his opportunity to climb over and live like a native. Melanie had tasted it briefly. She'd spent a few hours on the cusp of becoming a vampire. This was his turn, and he'd go all the way.

Dave knew that was the wolf talking. The hairy time bomb ticking away in his chest. He could feel the infection in his blood, making his veins itch. He didn't want to live for centuries. All that it meant was that you got to watch your loved ones die as you stood around helpless. What use was immortality if you're all alone? He'd just end up like Death. No, he had to halt the monster growing inside.

The first thing they needed to do, though, was get out of this room. With no other ideas, he tested the door handle.

'That doesn't sound like someone killing themselves,' came Martin's stern voice from the hallway. 'Sorry,' Dave called back. He turned to Melanie. 'We need to think. Put the kettle on.'

☾

After a couple of hours, all Dave and Melanie had accomplished was disassembling most of their hotel room. As far as they could see, there were no tools to use and no escape route. The sky had bruised and darkened, and they were all out of ideas.

'It's useless,' Melanie sighed.

'There has to be something,' Dave replied, stretched out over a bed covered in the contents of the wardrobe and cabinets. He clambered off the small hillock of stationery and coat hangers with the grace of a drunk man on a beanbag. There had to be a way out of here. This wasn't how he was meant to go. There was a new series of My Big Fat Geek Wedding starting on Netflix the following weekend. He searched the room one last time, looking for something, anything, that might lead to an escape plan. There was nothing.

'Okay. It's useless.'

Exhausted, Dave leaned back on the wall and suddenly, one of the wooden panels gave way with a quiet click. He probed the small gap between the slats, squeezing his fingers in until there was a pop and a crack, and a small hidden door swung open. It led to a small stone tunnel; the cold, damp air fogged with cobwebs and dust. It must be an old, forgotten priest hole, or some secret passage for previous residents to smuggle contraband - or people - in and out. Dave turned to Melanie, a triumphant glint in his eye. 'I bloody told you.' He pushed through webs veiling the entrance. 'Come on. We can still make it.' He could see Melanie hesitating. 'You trust me, don't you?'

Melanie smiled and nodded, but her hand wrapped itself around the letter opener which she hid up her sleeve.

☾

Dave and Melanie inched their way through the darkness, fingers exploring the rough, wet stone of the tunnel walls, until they came to a rickety ladder. Dave going first, they climbed down into the darkness one rotten rung at a time until they felt mossy ground underfoot. A slash of light guided them to the exit. A swift kick punctured the small wooden panel and the daylight poured in.

Melanie and Dave crawled out, the grey of the cobwebs caught in their hair, prematurely ageing them. Forced to squint against the light, it took a few seconds to realise they'd come out at the far side of the car park. Keeping low and using the other vehicles for cover, they scuttled towards the hire car. Dave fumbled the keys out of his pocket and pressed the remote's button, flinching as the alarm blipped and the car unlocked itself. He slipped into the driver's seat while Melanie scurried around and got into the passenger's side. Dave rammed the key into the car's ignition, but whenever he turned it the engine coughed, choked and died.

'They must have knackered the engine,' he groaned through gritted teeth, slapping the steering wheel with an open palm. He jumped out and reviewed the other vehicles lined up in the parking spaces. He settled on an old pickup truck that seemed to be held together by mud and the sheer willpower of the owner. 'Come on!' he ordered, sprinting as well as he was able to towards it. Melanie obeyed.

Trying the pickup's door, Dave was unsurprised to find it was unlocked. He swept the detritus of snack wrappers and drinks cans out onto the gravel and pulled himself up into the cabin. Melanie climbed in and over him, dragging herself over to the passenger side.

'Can you start this?' she asked, pulling a magazine from under her bottom. Dave pointed to the steering column where a set of keys hung from the ignition.

'It's a small, crime-free village, isn't it?' he said as he twisted the ignition switch. The truck's large engine choked and wheezed like a heavy smoker until it spluttered into life.

☾

'I spy with my little eye, something beginning with "C",' said Jack.

Martin rubbed his eyes with the balls of his hands. He wished he'd asked Dr Wilson for some painkillers before he'd left. 'If it's "carpet" again, I swear I'm going to--'

'Yes, it is. You should probably get more ornaments for this place,' Jack said. 'Your go!'

'I'm not in the mood.'

Jack pointed at the rifle leaning on the cracked leather arm of the sofa they sat on. 'You should just finish them with that.'

'I don't want blood on my hands,' Martin replied. 'This way, we get rid of our problem and the girl lives. He'll go down as another tragic suicide and nobody will believe anything she says if she mentions werewolves. It'll be the best for all concerned.'

Martin checked the weapon. It was true, he had no intention of using it, but it would be the simplest way to keep his two guests under control if they backed out of the plan. It'd been two hours and Dave must've done what was needed by now, but he wanted to give Melanie time to grieve. Perhaps

Dave's ghost would haunt the room in which he took his own life. A selfless gesture to save the lives of others. It was the least Dave could do after he ruined Martin's original marketing gimmick.

Martin had moved to Lunbridge ten years earlier. His dream had been to leave the rat race of the city behind and run a small boutique hotel. As soon as the first night, he could feel a presence in the building. He'd walk into a room and he would see his breath chill on the air even though it was a warm summer's day. Objects would move from place to place. After some research, he learned the story of Ophelia and Daniel and they soon found their way into the advertising literature.

Jack and Tommy became regulars and, quickly after that, friends. It wasn't long until Martin learned of Tommy's dark secret. Once every lunar cycle, the village's doors would be locked and the locals would get some reading done while he ran through the fields. At least he was good at sorting out the pests in the local farms.

Martin always thought there was a risk that something like this would happen. If he'd had his way, he'd have put a silver bullet through Tommy's heart years ago and ended the monthly torment. In fact, he'd had some made by a specialist gunsmith which he'd kept in the hotel's safe, just in case, but Jack wouldn't hear of it. Besides, it didn't make the best business sense to go around killing your customers. So, he held nothing against Dave and Melanie personally. It was them, or Tommy and--

An old engine coughed and spluttered into life in the car park below the window. Jack's ears pricked up.

'Is that my truck?'

☾

Carter and his lookout partner ran across the lawn towards the car park. Dave tried to think of the other man's name. It began with a 'K'. Keith? Kevin? Yeah, that probably wasn't the thing to be focusing on right now. Angered that Melanie and Dave had fooled them, they swore and shook their fists. Dave slammed the gearstick into reverse and stamped on the accelerator pedal. The pickup rocketed backwards and lurched round to face the exit. Wheelspinning out of the car park, they sprayed the pursuers with gravel and fishtailed out onto the road, just as Martin and Jack crashed through the hotel's doors. Dave was slow to crunch through the first few gears; he'd driven nothing this large before, but the hotel soon disappeared from the rearview mirror. Dave relaxed the more the distance from the hotel increased and allowed himself a sigh of relief.

But the sigh turned right back round and re-entered Dave's body as a gasp when a truck appeared behind them. Martin and Jack were looking cross in the cabin and there was an angry mob in the cargo bay.

'Must go faster,' said Melanie, who'd noticed they were being followed. Dave dropped down the gears and found an extra kick of speed from the engine.

They'd left the village and the jumbled blocks of cottages had been replaced by a smear of green and brown whipping past the windows.

Dave's senses had never been so sharp, his eyesight never so clear. Though the narrow road dipped and turned, the truck followed its path, cutting through the rolling hills. He expertly steered the truck around bends and sharp corners as if they were travelling on rails. His confidence bubbled until he thought it would burst up out of him. Their pursuers weren't making any ground on them and, as sure as night follows day, he knew they would escape.

Dave's metabolism was shot-gunning adrenaline. He'd always lived his life in a fog of self-doubt, but at this moment it had burned away and it seemed there wasn't anything he couldn't accomplish. He pushed his full weight down on the accelerator pedal and the pickup juddered forward. Melanie leaned over and placed a hand over his, which was welded to the gearstick.

'Take it easy,' she said, her tone a warning. Melanie's voice brought Dave back from the brink of mania. He eased off the pedals and took a deep breath as his body changed down the gears along with the truck. These roads were unfamiliar and dangerous. It'd be no use if he crashed into a--

The bend in the road was upon them quicker than Dave had expected and he slammed on the brakes with both feet. The verge dropped away and they instantly knew that this was the cliff face where they'd found the dead sheep.

Time ran in fast-forward and slow motion simultaneously. Dave saw each action both in pinpoint detail and as an indistinct blur. The pickup's tyres locked up as it slid across the road, whipping from side to side, throwing Dave and Melanie around like rag dolls. The vehicle left a trail of acrid smoke and melted rubber as it left the road. Melanie screamed and Dave grappled with the steering wheel, desperately trying to turn back onto the tarmac. It was no use, though, and they were thrown forward as the pickup dropped into a ditch and buried its front grille into the trunk of a large tree with a loud crunch.

Ken. That was the guy's name, Dave thought to himself as he blacked out for the second time in twenty-four hours.

☾

Martin pulled the Land Rover over to the side of the road. The pickup listed to one side like a wounded animal, the axle shattered. The fury of the chase over, the only sound was the creak of crumpled metal and the cooling of overheated engines, ticking like a countdown to something terrible.

He jumped down from the driver's seat and scrambled through the long grass to reach the wreckage. Melanie and Dave were semi-conscious, still strapped tightly to their seats, their heads lolling loosely, a fine spray of fresh blood across the spider-webbed windscreen. Martin tugged at the driver's door handle but it had warped shut. Carter and Ken helped Jack across the undulating terrain between the two vehicles and peered curiously through the pickup's window. Dave's head rolled back, and he stared out at them with glassy eyes.

'Oh, hi Ken,' he croaked before slipping away again.

Martin's gaze drifted from the pickup to the cliff's edge to the Land Rover and back again. 'Get the winch,' he ordered Ken, who stroked his beard nervously.

'W-w-what do you want that for, Martin?'

Martin's smile chilled Ken's blood. 'You know this road, Ken. It's treacherous. An accident black spot you shouldn't negotiate at speed in these conditions. It's too easy to take this corner too fast. Many have and paid the price. It's a pity these two impetuous youngsters, drunk on avocado and legal highs, didn't heed our warnings. So tragic. They'd barely experienced all the wonders life offered.'

Martin wanted this to end now. He'd given Dave the opportunity to take the dignified way out, but he'd been impolite enough to refuse it. He hadn't kept his word. Now somebody was just going to have to roll their sleeves up and get their hands dirty and if it had to be Martin, then so be it. A sacrifice was needed for the greater good.

Also, Dave was starting to really annoy him.

'What about the girl?' Jack asked, horrified. 'You can't kill her.'

'She's a witness to all of this,' Martin replied. 'And she'll be the first to go if he changes. She's dead, either way, and this involves the least number of questions. I'm just being practical.'

Ken nodded and beckoned Carter to follow him. They both trudged back to the Land Rover.

'She killed Tommy,' Martin said to Jack when the other two were out of earshot. 'You told me when I first came here. We're a close community. When one of our own is hurt, we sort it out amongst ourselves.'

They locked eyes. Something had changed in Martin and Jack could see it in the steely gaze that seemed to bore through him. He looked to the ground, defeated, offering his submission like a pack animal.

The Land Rover rumbled into life. Carter backed it away from the verge, towards the safety barrier, until it blocked most of the narrow road. Ken guided him with hand signals until he was close to the edge. A simple slap on the wheel arch with a palm of a hand made Carter apply the brakes. They were practical men, and both saw this as a simple piece of manual labour to dispose of a problem after which they could return to their normal lives. Ken grabbed the hook hanging from the winch attached to the front bumper and unwound the thick steel cable. He crossed back over the road, the cable snaking behind him, and crouched down to look for a sturdy piece of metal to secure the hook to.

'That truck's been good over the years,' Jack said, glum. Ken looked up from his work and nodded. They'd all be sad to see it go. He yanked the cable firmly to make sure he'd secured it.

'All set,' he called out to Carter before retreating to the Land Rover with the others. Martin looked at them.

'It's for the best,' he said, then switched the winch on.

☾

Dave woke slowly, consciousness teasing him from the dark cave of oblivion with the promise of higher brain function. There was a low rumble in the pit of his stomach and what seemed like a team of mice, squeaking angrily, had set to work on his brain with tiny pick axes.

'What the hell was I drinking?' he muttered before realising that, while the tiny pick axes were inside his head and the nausea swilled around his gut, the rumbling and squeaking was actually all around him.

Consciousness stopped being coy and grabbed Dave by the scruff of the neck. It flooded his senses. Information overload: Stop. Breathe. Process.

He was in a car wreck. Melanie next to him. The grey-black sky shifted above, which meant that the vehicle was moving backwards. That was the source of the noise; the rumble of the rough ground beneath the blown-out tyres and the squeal of twisted metal rubbing against itself.

There were voices now. Outside. 'That's as far as we can take it.' Martin. The reverberation stopped and Melanie stirred. 'We can use my car to push it over.' Push what over? Over what?

105

Oh no.

Dave shook Melanie awake. 'What happened?' she asked, her voice thick with confusion. 'Oh, yeah.'

'Are you okay?' Dave asked in an urgent whisper.

She nodded. 'Just banged about a bit.'

'We need to get out of here now.'

Melanie closed her eyes. 'Just five more minutes.'

Dave shook her again, with more force. 'Don't go to sleep. They're pushing us over the hillside.'

This brought Melanie around. She tried to open her door, but the crash had sealed it shut. Dave tugged at the handle on his side, but it wouldn't budge either. The engine of the other 4x4 started up and Dave watched it negotiate a tight three-point turn ahead of him. They only had seconds to live.

'If you're going to do something, now would be a good time,' Melanie said, a rabbit literally caught in headlights. Dave looked around the pickup's cabin for anything that might help them escape, but he couldn't think how some empty coffee cups and boiled sweets would save them. The Land Rover bared down on them, Martin behind the steering wheel, and the vehicles' bumpers slammed together. The engine complaining, Martin revved it higher, urging it on, until the wheels under them slid. Melanie reached out and clamped her hand around Dave's.

They travelled a few feet until the resistance of the safety barrier behind stopped them. It groaned against several tons of force until Dave heard the pop of a rivet. Then another. Defeated, he looked skyward. To his surprise, he felt a warmth beating down as if it was a summer's day. The moon had risen. Its power filled him, unknotting muscles and soothing the aches that had buried down to his bones.

He scooted over the gearstick until he was almost sat on Melanie's lap, lifting his feet up onto the driver's seat, and kicked out at the door, planting both heels into the panelling with all his strength. Nothing. He tried again, harder, until there was an almost imperceptible shift beneath his trainers. Metal screamed over his shoulder. The safety barrier had given way. With a final effort, Dave kicked the door one more time, and it popped away from the distorted frame. Melanie's hand still in his, he jumped from the pickup and dragged her with him as its back wheels slipped from the cliff's edge.

Landing hard, Melanie and Dave had a fraction of a second to watch the pickup disappear into the darkness below with a final roar. Martin, Jack, Carter and Ken had been so captivated by the spectacle of the pickup flipping down the steep mountainside that they hadn't noticed the escape occurring right under their noses. By the time they had, Dave and Melanie were on their feet and climbing up the steep bank on the other side of the road before disappearing down the incline.

☾

Dave didn't know how long they'd run for. He only knew of the surrounding air, the ground beneath his feet and, above, the endless sky burning with a billion suns. He was moon-drunk and he could run forever, naming every one of those stars as he did so, until he noticed a tug from behind.

'Must. Stop.' Melanie was on the verge of hyperventilating and Dave reluctantly came to a stop. His breath was deep too and, with every inhalation, his nose filled with her scent: Fear. He could hear her heart thumping arrhythmically in her chest; a drumbeat for a death march.

The loved ones are usually the first to be slaughtered.

'You have to get out of here.'

Melanie shook her head. 'I'm not leaving you. Besides, we're in the middle of nowhere. Where do you expect me to go?'

Dave's limbs twitched as if the molecules they were made from were trying to break the configuration they were set in. 'I'm feeling unusual.'

Melanie took two steps backwards. 'Are you going to--?'

'No, I'm fighting it. You know when you're going to throw up and you don't want to, and it's really hard but you put all your effort and concentration into not barfing?'

Melanie nodded. 'Well, it's like that but instead of puke it's a wolf.'

Melanie looked around and saw nothing but darkness in all directions. 'What are we going to do?'

Dave shrugged. 'Perhaps Martin was right. I should march straight back to that cliff and throw myself off. I don't want to spend the rest of my life a monster.'

'There's got to be another way.'

108

'Well, I'm taking any ideas because I'm all out.'

They both stood there, the chill breeze tugging at their clothes as if it was urging them in a certain direction, as they tried to think of a way out of the situation.

'I'll do it,' Melanie said, finally.

'What?'

She pulled out the silver letter opener she'd tucked into her jeans. 'I'll do it,' she repeated. 'If anyone should do it, it should be me. I'm not letting you kill yourself. I've spent my whole life being told that things do not end well for those who do, spiritually. It's silver so it should do the job.'

'Yeah, but look at that thing. It's blunt. I've got no idea how you stabbed Tommy with it.'

Melanie bent down and picked up a heavy-looking rock.

'Yeah, that should do it,' he said. This was the right thing to do. How many deaths would he be responsible for if he lived? Besides, he had an advantage over the rest of humanity; he knew what came after this even if it wasn't what most people thought it was. There'd been no middleman in a pulpit. He'd had the direct line.

But there were all those things he'd hoped to do; marrying Melanie and having children together for a start. Then embarrassing those children as they grew older together as a family. Could you regret the things that would never happen? Because that's what the gaping, empty chasm in his chest felt like. Still, it was for the greater good.

Dave kissed Melanie gently, tasting the saltiness of her tears. 'I love you,' she whispered.

'I know,' Dave replied. 'I'll make sure I come back and haunt you.'

A sad smile tugged at Melanie's lips. 'You better.'

'Tell Death where I am.' Dave unbuttoned his shirt, aware of how inappropriate its bright colours were in this moment. Melanie reached out and ran her fingers along his chest, which was hairier than usual, before giving him a gentle push. Dave did as he was told and laid down, the grass cool against his neck. As he stared up into the heavens, a certain peace enveloped him, as if he was falling asleep beneath the stars, as he had done so many times camping with his parents as a child. Perhaps he'd see them again soon. He would've loved to introduce Melanie to them.

Melanie knelt down by his side and slipped the letter opener's blade between the ribs guarding Dave's heart. Its cold, dull point repeatedly pressed into his skin as Melanie shook with the tears. 'I always knew you'd break my heart,' said Dave, trying to lighten the mood. A laugh slipped out through Melanie's crying. She looked to the rock in her fist, gauging its size, hoping her hand-to-eye coordination wouldn't let her down, and raised it above her head.

The rock.

'Gwyneth,' Melanie said with a smile.

Dave looked up at her. 'Paltrow? How's she going to help? I'm not putting crystals up anywhere.'

Melanie shook her head. 'Frost. The witches on the hill. The legend says they were the ones responsible for the original curse. Maybe, if we can free them, they can reverse the whole lycanthropy thing.'

'But only those truly in love can count the same number of stones twice,' Dave reminded her.

Melanie dropped the stone and letter opener. 'I think tonight has shown that we've got as good a chance as anybody else on that front.'

Dave shrugged. 'It's worth a go. I knew there was a reason I fell for you.'

'Do you think you can make it that far?'

Dave nodded and held his hand out for Melanie to help him to his feet, which she did.

'Which way is it?' he asked, wiping the mud and grass from his clothes. Melanie pointed in the direction the wind was blowing.

'That's the shortest route, but it means we'll have to go through Lunbridge.'

'Well, we'll just have to be sneaky. By the way, good use of the word "lycanthropy",' Dave said as they set off towards the hill.

Melanie smiled at the compliment. 'Thanks. I've been waiting to use it all night.'

☾

Move to the country, they said. *Leave the stress of city life behind you*, they said. What did they know? No matter how cutthroat the world of financial marketing became, Martin never once found himself loading silver ammunition into a rifle in the middle of the night. Sat in the small office behind the hotel's reception, he muttered to himself as he picked shiny bullets one by one from a small pile sat on a stack of VAT receipts and plugged them into the gun's magazine.

After Melanie and Dave had escaped, Martin had brought the others back to Lunbridge. If they were going out onto the moors during a full moon, they would need to be armed and well-equipped. Carter was down in the cellar locating torches, Ken had gone home to get his dog to track any scent trails their prey may have left behind, and Jack was helping himself to plenty of Dutch courage from the shelves behind the bar.

The rifle loaded, Martin rammed the bolt home and set the safety catch on. He closed the safe and put the remaining ammunition in his jacket. His pockets jangling with a deathly melody, he went through to the bar where Carter was checking the supplies he'd found and Jack was negotiating his third whisky. He was definitely looking braver than when Martin had left him. He carefully placed the rifle on the bar, grabbed a glass from a shelf and poured himself a shot, throwing the drink back in one.

'Is that stuff okay?' he asked wheezily, wiping his eyes. Carter shrugged and picked up a torch, flicking the switch on and off, bouncing frantic morse code signals off the brass hanging from the walls.

'They make light. So I'd say, yes.'

The pub door opened with a rattle and Ken led his dog into the bar. Martin looked at the animal with bemusement.

'That's your dog?' he asked.

'Yes,' Ken confirmed with a proud smile. 'Cost me a fortune.'

'It's a poodle.' It was. In fact, it was the most poodley thing he'd ever seen. It even had a little puffy tail.

'Yeah, the wife always wanted one.'

'What's its name?' Martin asked as the dog buried its muzzle into his crotch.

'*Her* name. She's Princess Gigi Trixibelle.'

Princess Gigi Trixibelle licked her adorable wet nose. Martin could feel his headache returning. 'And you think this is an appropriate animal to track down a werewolf?'

'Oh, yeah. Poodles are very underrated as trackers. She's vicious when she wants to be. You should see what she did to the duvet in the spare bedroom. Besides, Dave won't be a great werewolf, it being his first time 'n' all.'

Always one to make the best of a bad situation, Martin forced a smile. 'Right, well, we'd better go up to their room and see if we can find something for her to pick up the scent from.'

☾

Being in love was difficult. If one of you wasn't complaining that the washing up had been left in the sink, then one was trying to stab the other through

113

the heart with a blade of silver to stop you from turning into a supernatural creature of the night. *That would be one for the relationships subreddit if he and Melanie ever made it back to London (and reliable broadband)*, Dave thought as they walked back to Lunbridge in awkward silence.

The village was quiet, but still he and Melanie kept to the shadows, pressed up to whitewashed walls and peering around corners before scurrying to the next shelter. Soon, they found themselves outside the church. Shadows carved into the gothic architecture and the blood-red stains on the glass made it less inviting than their first visit, but the sound of voices in the dark forced them forward.

'Let's hide in here,' Melanie whispered urgently. 'If nothing else, surely the vicar will help us.' She grabbed Dave's hand, and he allowed himself to be guided up the path through the gravestones. They pushed the heavy oak door open and crept into the church.

Reverend Peter, knelt at the altar in prayer, turned on hearing the creaking wood and smiled. He slowly got to his feet and rubbed his knees. 'Oof. That's a long way up,' he groaned. He hobbled over to the two visitors, taking in their bloody clothes and beaten-up bodies. 'Please, take a seat. It looks as if you've had a rough night.'

'Thank you,' Melanie said as she and Dave collapsed onto a pew in the middle of the nave. 'We're sorry for disturbing you,'

Peter waved the apology away as he pushed the heavy door closed. 'Quite all right, my dear. I was praying for poor Thomas's soul. Such a terrible business. I can only hope, in death, he finds the peace he could never find in life.' He smiled at the pair. 'It's rare to have two so young visit so often. What brings you here tonight?'

'Well... Err--' Melanie stuttered. She couldn't lie to a man of the cloth, but also didn't feel much like telling him the truth.

'Are you looking for forgiveness?' Peter looked at Dave and his smile grew cold. 'Or should I be praying for your soul, too?'

Dave clambered to his feet. 'Thanks very much for the sanctuary and all that, but I think we need to be getting on.'

Peter turned the iron key in the door's lock. 'Oh, I can't let you leave. What would my parishioners think if I let a new monster loose on them so soon after they were rid of the previous one?'

'Look, I don't know what you've heard but we have a plan,' Dave said. 'If we can just get to the stones and free the witches--'

Peter cut him off. 'Those pagan rituals will do you no good. My mission is to keep this village safe.' He reached down and picked something heavy and wooden that had been leaning on the stone wall by the door. At first, it looked like a cross or crucifix to Dave. He only realised it was a crossbow when the vicar pointed the silver-tipped arrow directly at Dave's heart.

'You have got to be shitting me!' Dave blurted out.

'Dave!' Melanie scolded.

'Let's be reasonable here,' Dave said to Peter. 'Doesn't it say thou shalt not kill in the bible?'

'The needs of the many outweigh the needs of the few.'

'Where does it say that in the bible?' Melanie asked.

'It's Star Wars,' Peter replied.

'Star *Trek*,' Dave corrected. He looked at Melanie. 'Seriously, when people get them mixed up, it's like a knife in the heart.'

'That's the spirit,' Peter said as he re-aimed the crossbow. Then, in a calm, steady voice, he said, 'The Lord is my shepherd. I shall not want.'

Dave dived to the side, pulling Melanie down with him, as Peter pulled the trigger. The arrow buried itself in the wooden chair where they'd just been sat, showering them with splinters as they lay on the cold stone floor between two rows of pews.

'He makes me to lie down in green pastures,' Peter continued, his voice echoing around the nave. 'He leads me beside the still waters.'

His footsteps approached where Dave and Melanie were hiding. 'He's got to reload,' she hissed. 'Go and get him.'

'I'm not punching a priest!' Dave whispered in reply. He pointed to the aisle running along the far wall. 'Shift down there.' Crawling on their hands and knees, they headed away from Peter's voice.

'He restores my soul. He leads me in the paths of righteousness, for His name's sake.'

Dave and Melanie reached the end of the pew and Dave risked a quick glance over at Peter. He was already fixing a new arrow to the crossbow and pulling back the string. When it was locked in place, he breathed deeply and said, 'Yea, though I walk through the valley of the shadow of death, I will fear no evil.'

He sprinted the last few feet to where he thought Dave and Melanie were hiding, aimed and fired the arrow. It bounced harmlessly off the stone floor as Dave shoved the pew with all his strength, smashing it into Peter and sending him flying. Before he'd hit the ground, Dave and Melanie were on their feet and running for the door.

Dave wrestled with the key, his sweat-and-blood smeared hands making it difficult to get a grip, until the lock popped open and he flung the door wide. Melanie followed him out into the night before she turned around and grabbed the key. She pulled the door tightly shut and locked it behind her.

'Why, wherever we go, do people try to kill us?' Melanie asked as she threw the key into a bush.

'It must be my winning personality,' Dave replied. 'I can only assume it's things like this are the reason fewer people are going to church.'

☾

Soon Dave and Melanie were back at the Half Moon Inn. They'd just need to cross the road and they would be in the fields with a clear run to the hill where the stones stood. They took cover behind a well-trimmed hedge. Dave was glad of the rest. Even though it was a cool night, he was sweating as his body fought against the infection. His bones felt like badly-constructed flatpack furniture, as if one slipped bolt would cause his entire skeleton to unravel.

'I think the coast's clear,' Melanie whispered to him, her body pressed up against Dave's. He was glad she hadn't abandoned him like he'd told her to. She had a big heart. A big, juicy heart, a succulent liver and soft flesh and-- *Stop it, Dave.* He gritted his teeth until the craving had passed.

'Are you okay?' Melanie asked, concerned. Dave nodded.

'Let's just get there.' They crawled out from the hedge and, crouched low, scuttled like insects across the road. They'd almost made it to the safety of the meadows when a voice called out behind them.

'Hello?'

Dave turned around. A naked man stood in the middle of the road. Tommy. Why did the dead always show up at the worst times?

'Melanie!' he hissed, and her head appeared from the bushes behind him.

'What's wrong?' Dave gestured to, what looked like to her, a deserted road.

'Tommy's here.'

'Tom--? Oh. Right,' she replied when it finally clicked. Dave scanned the hotel's windows, but there was no movement behind them.

'Wait here.' He stood up slowly and approached Tommy, keeping his gaze above waist-height. Dave didn't know why ghosts were always dressed, or not, in the clothes they had died in. Perhaps it was a residual projection of the self, or a filter that allowed those that could see them process it. Death told him once about two actors who were struck by a falling stage light and died. If that wasn't tragic enough, they'd been dressed as a pantomime horse at the time. Dave had hoped the one at the back didn't have to spend eternity with his head up his friend's bottom. As he crossed the road, Dave realised that he'd narrowly escaped spending the whole afterlife wearing the shirt Melanie hated. That was a close call.

'Oh, it's you,' Tommy said as Dave came closer. 'Sorry about the-- ' he trailed off and pointed at the bandage poking under the collar of Dave's shirt.

'You remember what you did?'

'Yeah. It's like you're trapped in the back seat of a car being driven by a maniac. You're aware of everything he's doing, but you can't grab the wheel and you can't put the brakes on.' Tommy sighed. 'You'll find out soon enough. Can you feel it yet?'

Dave nodded. 'I'm scared.'

'So you should be. Still, you'll get used to it.'

'Really?'

'No, but you'll soon realise what dates you can't hold your monthly book club meetings, or whatever you city folk get up to.' Tommy looked over Dave's shoulder. 'Is that your girl hiding back there? You should tell her to get as far away from you as possible. The loved ones are usually the first to get slaughtered.'

'So people keep telling me.'

Tommy looked down at his own naked body. 'Though, obviously, she can look after herself.'

'Yeah, she's sorry about that.'

Tommy shrugged. 'I've had a good innings. It had to happen sooner or later. But, killed by a girl. How embarrassing.' He shook his head, disappointed.

Dave pointed a finger in Tommy's face. 'Hey, dude. That's my girlfriend. It's the twenty-first century. She's a strong, independent woman who's more than capable of slaying werewolves, vampires, or any other undead entity.'

'Thanks, babe,' Melanie called out from the undergrowth.

Tommy rolled his eyes. 'Snowflake.'

'So, what's your plan, then?' Tommy asked, scratching his crotch.

'Can you not do that, please? It's really off-putting,' Dave said, waving at Tommy's groin. 'We're going to the standing stones. See if we can wake Gwyneth and her daughters.'

Tommy let out a low whistle which made Dave wonder how he could do that seeing as there was no air for him to blow. 'When a man is putting his faith in witches, then he's really run out of ideas.'

'Well, you don't seem to have come up with anything better.'

'Don't get me wrong, there were women over the years and some of those I thought I loved. I told them as much. I'd march right up to the top of that hill and try to count the stones, but it never worked.' Tommy sighed. 'I've hurt many people in every way imaginable. Now, here I am, doomed to walk the earth with my tackle out forever. I've been cursed in life and now I'm cursed in death.'

'I can help you out with that.'

'Really? I was wondering why you could see me when the others couldn't.'

'What others?'

'Oh, my brother, Martin, and a couple of the other fellas. Looked to be in a hurry.'

'Right. We'd better get a move on, then.'

'Fair enough. Just give me a second.' Tommy stared at the moon sitting fat and ripe in the inky black midnight sky. 'You know, this is the first time in I don't know how long I've looked up there without fear.' With a smile, he turned to look at Dave.

'I'm ready now.'

☾

This was it. Dave had nothing more to give. They'd made it out of the village and had crossed field and forest to get this far, but every step now felt like he was walking across the ocean bed in shoes made of concrete. He fell to his knees, throwing his hands out to stop falling forward, the thick mud cool against his burning skin. With great effort, he raised his head. Melanie continued to march up the hill to the standing stones; still nothing more than dark marks scratched into the moon behind them. They'd failed and all they could do now was to avoid joining the list of couples that met a sticky end in this place.

'Melanie,' Dave called out, his voice barely a croak. Melanie turned to see him collapse to the ground. She ran back to help, but he waved her away with a limp hand. He no longer had the strength to lift his head to look at her.

'I need you to do something for me,' he gasped through hacking breaths.

'What?'

Dave's head whipped up with newfound energy and he stared back at her with hungry eyes. A snarl danced at the corner of his lips.

'RUN.'

☾

'Do you really have to carry that dog?' Martin asked, exasperated. He, Ken and Carter were half-way up the hill and he was thinking they'd never find Dave and Melanie. They'd decided it would be best to leave Jack in the pub, partly in case Melanie and Dave returned, but mostly because he'd got through the best part of a bottle of whisky before they left. Maybe he had the right idea and they should all go back, wait the night out and deal with whatever remained of Melanie in the morning - along with their hangovers.

Ken carried Princess Gigi Trixibelle in his arms. 'Have you seen how muddy it is round here? The wife would kill me. She only gave her a bath yester-day. I'll just point her towards Dave's scent. Here, watch this.'

The three stopped and Ken turned in a slow circle until Princess Gigi Trixibelle wagged her tail. 'There. That way.' He and Carter struck out in the direction the dog had indicated. Martin shook his head and, shifting the rifle strap strung over his shoulder, followed the other two.

'I feel under-equipped,' Carter said. 'Shouldn't we be carrying burning torches, or something? Isn't that traditional?'

'I think it would be best if we continued in silence,' Martin replied.

Then, a scream ripped through the still night air ahead of them. They scanned the hillside until Martin spotted two figures in the distance. 'Werewolf!'

'Where wolf?'

Martin pointed into the darkness. 'There wolf!'

☾

Dave got to his feet unsteadily. 'Oh, man. This will sting a bit,' he said through gritted teeth before doubling over in agony. Melanie looked on in shock as bones moved and slid under his skin, reshaping and regrouping in new, inhuman formations. Muscle and flesh contorted, tearing the shirt from his back, as thick hair sprouted along his spine. There was a sickening cracking sound as limbs lengthened, growing heavier and stronger.

It was his face, though, that truly horrified Melanie. His jaw dislocated with a pop, his now-monstrous mouth quickly filling with razor-sharp teeth. His skull shifted impossibly, becoming elongated and wedge-shaped. She watched as the man she loved disappeared, the humanity fading from his eyes and his pale skin disappearing under dense hair. Dave's screams and groans deepened until they gave way to heavy, bestial growling. Then, as suddenly as it began, the transformation was complete and a snarling wolf clawed the ground. It took a few seconds for Melanie to realise that the only one left screaming was her.

The wolf took an unsteady step forward, using his new limbs for the first time. He snarled and bared his teeth. Hunger was something he was already familiar with. Melanie was about to close her eyes to await the inevitable when a bright light flashed in the dark below accompanied by a crack that rattled around the hillside. A red gash appeared on the wolf's flank and he fell to the ground, flailing and yelping in pain. Somebody was shooting at them.

Melanie took advantage of the distraction and ran for the top of the hill. She told herself to not look back. She would only have one chance. She concentrated on the stones ahead of her, calculating the ever-decreasing distance as they grew larger. The sound of the blood roaring in her ears meant she had no idea if she was being pursued; whether Dave had escaped, or if it was all too late and the villagers had hit their target. She ignored that last option and continued onwards until the air scalded her lungs and her muscles burned like fire. The seconds stretched out and it seemed like she would never make it to the top. Then, finally, the standing stones were on top of her. Melanie collapsed, gulping down lung-fuls of air even though every breath was agony. There was no time to rest, so she staggered to her feet. Moonlight bathed the hilltop and the stones gave off an ethereal glow. Despite her fear, she could feel there was magic all around her.

A low growl behind her brought her back to the problem at hand. She turned to face the wolf stood at the edge of the circle of stones. Its black fur ren-dered it almost invisible; nothing but a set of teeth and eyes hovering in the dark. It took a step forward into the silver light, then whimpered like a puppy and retreated. Something kept the beast at bay. Melanie had never seen a wolf baffled before, but its expression was familiar. If she looked carefully, Dave was in there somewhere, the gears shifting be-hind the eyes. It was the same look of befuddled confusion when he couldn't find his phone, or he didn't understand the ending of a movie. Even his fur looked unmanageable. She allowed herself a small smile. This gave Melanie the resolve she needed. She moved through the stones, counting each one off loudly, ignoring the wolf patiently pac-ing around the periphery of the stone circle. She believed this would work; that she would save the man she loved with basic arithmetic. More ridicu-lous things had happened during the last few months. As she moved around the outcrop of stones, the wolf padded alongside her. Sometimes he fol-lowed like an obedient pet, and sometimes he stalked her like the hunter instinct was telling him to.

'Get away from him, Melanie,' a voice called out behind her. Martin stood on the outskirts of the circle, the rifle pointed at the prowling wolf. Keeping one eye on the stone she'd just counted, Melanie stepped forward, putting herself between the two.

'No,' she said in her bravest voice. The wolf growled a warning, pawing the dirt, ready to charge.

'Goddamn it, girl,' Martin barked in frustration. 'Get out of the way and we can finish this.'

'No,' she repeated, her tone more certain. Martin shuffled to his right, circling the edge of the hilltop. Melanie moved with him, shielding the wolf. 'Where are the others?'

Martin shrugged, keeping the rifle trained on her. 'Well, they're not as young as they used to be. I had to leave them halfway down the hill.'

Out of the corner of her eye, Melanie thought she saw a rock move. 'Let me do this, Martin.'

'You're summoning the witches?' He spat, incredulous. 'It's an old wives' tale.'

'I have to try.' Melanie pointed at the next rock. 'Thirty-two. Thirty-three. Thirty-four.' She looked around, sure she'd accounted for all the stones. She counted again from the side she began. 'One.'

The wolf and Martin continued to orbit around Melanie, all three moving in a slow dance of death. She continued to count aloud, mentally ticking off each rock and boulder as she stepped around them. Often she would hesitate, afraid she'd lost count, but then continued on, the numbers climbing ever higher. Sometimes, Martin would try to trick her, changing direction when her line of sight was blocked or shouting out random numbers to confuse her, but she was prepared for his chicanery. Soon, the end was in sight.

'Thirty-three.' Victorious, she looked across the hilltop to Martin, a pithy comment already prepared, and saw him smiling.

'Wha--?' she asked when, out of the corner of her eye, a large body charged towards her. For a fraction of a second, she worried that the wolf had found a way into the circle, but then she realised it was the heavy frame of Ken. He knocked her to the ground, clearing Martin's line of sight, and screamed, 'Shoot him, Martin!'

At the sound of Ken's voice, the wolf sprinted around the perimeter of the circle, his teeth bared, covering the ground between him and Martin. Martin levelled the rifle and trained it on the wolf, looking for one clean shot. Disorientated, Melanie struggled to her feet, frantically trying to remember which rock she'd got to. She could see the distance between the wolf and Martin rapidly decreasing. The hunter and the prey. But which one was which? It wouldn't matter. It would be over soon. This wasn't where The Tale of Melanie and Dave ended, she told herself. They wouldn't be joining the list of doomed lovers. Not just yet, anyway. There was so much more to tell. Horror. Romance...

Comeback story.

Melanie pointed a steady finger at a dark brown, moss-encrusted rock at her feet. 'Thirty-four.'

The ground shook, tipping Martin backwards as he pulled the trigger, and the bullet disappeared harmlessly into the night. The wolf stopped and sniffed the dirt inquisitively. When Melanie's ears had stopped ringing from the sound of the rifle, a low hum filled the air. She walked over to the tallest stone and placed a hand on it. A subtle vibration travelled the length of her arm, increasing in magnitude until a crack split its rough surface. Then another, like an ancient egg hatching. Lights emanated all around her from inside the stones themselves. Shadows moved as layers slid off the megaliths like a peeling onion, crashing to the ground and splintering.

'What the hell's going on?' Martin shouted above the cacophony.

'I think Gwyneth's waking up!' Melanie told him with a laugh. The wolf trotted through the rocks and dust, sniffing the debris as if searching for something.

With a final burst of light, the earthquake stopped as suddenly as it had begun. Melanie blinked away the glow seared onto her optic nerves and, when her vision cleared, a tall woman with a kind smile stood in front of her.

'How long was I in there? My feet are bloody killing me,' she said.

☾

The hilltop was busier than the height of the tourist season as figures woke from centuries of slumber.

128

Melanie counted thirteen, from young girls to old women, all dressed in long black dresses greyed by the dust swirling in the air. They hugged and sobbed, finally free from their stone prisons. Martin had dropped the rifle and wandered around them in a daze, muttering to himself.

'Are you Gwyneth?' Melanie asked the woman.

'That I be,' she replied, brushing her skirt clean. 'Do we have you to thank for breaking the curse?'

'Yes, I suppose so. I'm Melanie.' She held her hand out awkwardly. 'Big fan of your work.'

Gwyneth shook her hand gently. 'Then thank you, Melanie.' There was that smile again, warm as a summer evening. The wolf strutted over and sat at Gwyneth's feet, licking her hand as affectionately as a puppy. 'And what's your name?' she asked.

'Dave,' Melanie replied for him.

'Dave?' Gwyneth repeated. 'A fine name for a fine animal.' She took the wolf's head in both hands, gazing deep into its eyes. She looked back at Melanie. 'I take it this is the recipient of the love that freed us?'

Melanie nodded. 'Is there anything you can do? He's more of a cat person.'

Gwyneth laughed. 'Are you sure? I find a dog is a lot more loyal and of more use than a man even if it's just once a month. But, yes, it would be the least I could do. In the morning, I'll send one of my girls to fetch wolfsbane. Prepared correctly, it can reverse the curse of the werewolf. Tonight, though, I'd let him run free. He will return to you.' Princess Gigi Trixibelle bounded over, yapping constantly. She and the wolf introduced themselves by sniffing each other's behind. Melanie giggled.

'Oh, man. I hope he doesn't remember that.'

'How long were we trapped in the stones?' Gwyneth asked.

Melanie shifted uncomfortably. 'I don't know. Two or three hundred years?'

'Oh, I see. What's this century like?'

Melanie shrugged her shoulders. 'It's okay. Less dysentery and more snack food. Twiglets will blow your mind.'

'I see,' Gwyneth said. 'I feel I should greet my sisters after so long apart and then, perhaps, try a twiglet.'

'Of course,' Melanie replied. She left Gwyneth alone with the others and found Martin sat slack-jawed and dumbfounded on the remains of a boulder. Melanie gestured for him to move over and she joined him. They sat in silence, watching the scenes of joy.

'I'm sorry,' he said finally.

'You were doing what you thought you had to do. We won't be coming back here though... What with the attempted murder and everything.'

'Understandable. Are you going to involve the authorities?'

'And tell them what exactly?'

'Three-star review, then?' Martin nodded towards the wolf following Gwyneth wherever she went. 'Is he going to be all right?'

'Yeah, I think he's too in love with Gwyneth to do anyone any harm and they can fix him in the morning.' Melanie put a hand on Martin's shoulder. 'Are you going to be okay?'

Martin looked at her, amused. 'Are you kidding me? There's a coven of witches in town. I will make a fortune.'

MONDAY

When Melanie had hugged the wolf goodbye and let him run off down the hillside, everybody with three legs or fewer returned to the Half Moon Inn. Gwyneth and her sisters had their first girls' night out in almost three centuries. Martin was the perfect host, providing drinks and snacks throughout the night, while Melanie brought them up to speed with world events from the time they were petrified up to the present day. In hindsight, she probably concentrated a bit too much on what was going on in Grey's Anatomy, but she'd been bingeing it before coming away for the weekend and they *did* all seem interested in whether Meredith and McDreamy worked things out.

Soon the dawn chorus heralded the rising of the sun and Melanie's gaze focussed on the door, as if she could make Dave walk through it through sheer force of will. Soon, her wish was granted and he stood there, naked and smeared with dirt. There was still a wild look in his eyes, twigs and leaves entwined in his hair like a rudimentary crown.

In Melanie's opinion, he'd never looked better. She ran from the table, kicking her chair over, and hugged and peppered him with kisses. 'I love you,' she whispered into his grubby ear. He looked back at her, dazed and confused.

'Aren't you going to say anything?' she asked, worried that the night had irrevocably broken him. Dave opened and shut his mouth silently as if trying to kick-start his brain. After a while, he formed the words he was looking for.

'Was I sniffing a dog's arse?'

☾

'Will they be okay?' Dave asked, staring out of the passenger window of the hire car.

'Who?' Melanie asked, hunched forward over the steering wheel, concentrating on the procession of cars in front.

'Gwyneth and her mates.'

Melanie shrugged. 'Martin said he'd help get them settled. Some of them still have descendants living in the area. They'll be fine. We've already got a WhatsApp group set up and we're planning a night out.'

'God help us all.'

'Shut up and drink your wolfsbane. Gwyneth went to all that effort to make it for you.'

Dave sipped from a travel flask, shuddering at the bitter taste. 'Martin told me what you did. Putting yourself between me and him. Thank you.'

'What else could I do? I've got attached to you. It's the classic tale. Boy meets girl. Boy loses girl. Girl becomes vampire. Boy saves girl. Boy becomes werewolf. Girl saves boy.'

'A story as old as time. Aren't we meant to be mortal enemies or something now?'

'Don't believe everything you see in the movies.'

Dave closed his eyes. The hum of the motorway traffic, the soundtrack to his return to civilisation, soothed him. His memory of the night before was hazy. Yes, he did a very bad job of chasing after a flock of sheep and he was pretty sure they were mocking him at one point. But apart from that, there was a sense of freedom, running through the forest and fields under the spring moon, that he'd never experienced before. He'd slipped the bonds of the human world and had been part of something bigger. It was a sensation he would never forget. 'Maybe I'll start jogging again when my shoulder's healed,' he said.

He'd woken in a clearing, naked and cold but exhilarated, and had made his way back to the pub where he'd showered and dressed. By the time he'd made himself feel more human, Carter had fixed the hire car and Gwyneth was already in the kitchen cooking up a cure. She assured him it would remove all traces of lycanthropy from his system, except perhaps he'd prefer his meat cooked rarer from now on.

They'd said goodbye to their new friends and set off for London. Now, Dave relaxed as he watched the city swell and rise in front of him. It was true, absence made the heart grow fonder. They left the motorway and soon Melanie was parallel parking in front of the tired old Victorian flat they called home. Dave smiled.

'I think life's going to be easier from now on. Vampires. Werewolves. What else left is there?'

As they unpacked, a man wobbled up to Dave. He was in his mid-thirties, with matted blonde hair and he was dressed in a tatty plaid shirt and jeans. He looked like he hadn't slept in days. This guy had obviously had an interesting weekend too.

'Excuse me,' he croaked.

'What's up?' Dave asked, strangely comforted by the return of the anxiety that came with urban living.

'You've got to help me, Dave.' Dave looked him up and down. He didn't remember him; and he looked like someone who'd be memorable if you ran into him.

'I'm sorry, do I know you?'

'It's me. It's Death,' the man replied, fear in his eyes. 'I've had a little accident.'

AUTHOR'S NOTE

Even though the story you've just read has ended on a horrible cliffhanger, this is the end of a little era. Once upon a time, I had an idea for a series of novellas telling the story of Death and the problems he had trying to sort out the undead. Each would play with the tropes of the horror/fantasy genre; ghost stories, vampires, zombies, Lovecraftian horror and werewolves.

'I'll bash them out over a year or two,' I thought. 'It'll be a nice little project to keep me out of trouble.'

It's five years later and I'm finally done.

So now I've spent over half a decade getting that out of my system, there's still a big bunch of stories I want to tell about this little universe I've scribbled into existence. Big stories. So goodbye novellas, hello novels that'll delve deeper into the lives and histories of these characters I spend most of my day with.

And I've made a plan. It'll be a lot quicker this time round.

Honest.

But, at this point of the journey, there are some people I really need to thank:

Everyone who supported me on Kickstarter from the beginning--I wouldn't have done this without you. You rock.

If you've tweeted, or Facebooked or blogged about them–You, too, are awesome.

If you've got in touch with me to tell me you've enjoyed my writing, thank you. You don't know how much that means and how much it helps when it's the middle of the night and I can't think of that last joke for the scene.

Or if you've simply read them and not told people that they sucked.

And my wife (who probably won't read this), who has looked on me doing this with a mixture of bewilderment and patience. She knew I had to do this even if she'll never really understand why. I love her very much. She puts up with a lot.

And my kids (who I won't let read this). If it wasn't for the Three Infinite Monkeys, these books would've probably been written a lot quicker but the gaps in between wouldn't have been even a tenth as much fun.

Death Will Return.

All the best,

Dave
December 2018

Printed in Great Britain
by Amazon

79675101R00082